MY NAME IS RAND

MY NAME IS RAND

THE CLASSIC EROTIC NOVEL BY WAYNE COURTOIS

THE LIBRARY OF HOMOSEXUAL CONGRESS

NEW ORLEANS & NEW YORK

Published in the United States of America by
REBEL SATORI PRESS
www.rebelsatoripress.com

Cover photo by nito
Book design by Sven Davisson

ISBN:978-1-60864-317-2

INTRODUCTION: THE NAKED RAND

By Jerry L. Wheeler

When Wayne Courtois asked me to write the introduction to this, the third edition of his groundbreaking tickle torture novel, *My Name Is Rand*, I jumped at the opportunity. Not only do I get to promote smut, but I also get to extol its virtues as serious writing. Because who says it can't be both? Not me.

And, apparently, not Courtois either—who admits the genesis of *My Name Is Rand* was humble "one-handed enjoyment," as he calls it, for both himself and a small group of tickling enthusiasts. The book was the outgrowth of a few tickling short stories written as far back as 1982 as well as an outrageous torture novella called *Ten Apologies* picked up by publishers Greg Wharton and Ian Phillips for Wharton's webzine, *Suspect Thoughts: A Journal of Subversive Writing*. Wharton wanted more, so Courtois sent him *Rand*.

"When we read *My Name Is Rand* we said yes right away to publishing it with Suspect Thoughts Press," said Wharton. "How could we not with a tale so dark, perversely suspenseful, and deeply, painfully erotic?" Unfortunately, the book became unavailable when Suspect Thoughts Press folded. It was picked up for a second edition but then went out of print again and remained so until Tom Cardamone recently selected it for rebirth through The Library of Homosexual Congress, an imprint of Rebel Satori Press (Sven Davisson, Publisher).

I thought I had read *Rand* for my blog *Out in Print: Queer Book Reviews* when the short-lived second edition came out in 2010, but I must have read the Suspect Thoughts edition, because the review was actually written by one of my guest reviewers, George Seaton, who indicated that at its core, *My Name Is Rand* is a book about the rewards and perils of self-discovery. I can't argue with that assessment.

Rand is a knowledge-seeker intent on hooking up with a man named Granger, an ex-Navy man who's equally intent to fulfill Rand's desire to be tickled to death. Or at least to orgasm. After his weekend with Granger, he leaves to rejoin his partner, David, but has another tickling encounter on the way home at a roadside rest stop with a guy named Michael, who kidnaps Rand and spirits him away to a mysterious place called the Compound.

The Compound, an early name for the book, is where men, women, and children alike form a gruesome gauntlet of tickling devices and tortures practiced on the helpless inmates, who are guided and attended by trustees. Rand eventually becomes one of these trustees and has a supernatural encounter with the boss Dred Junior before joining the rebel side to overthrow the unseen commanders of the Compound.

Yes. It's a ride.

Courtois is a superb writer who has a strong narrative intuition that drives this story to destinations you wouldn't normally think of. And this is his personal fetish, so he writes with the gusto of an ardent enthusiast, and that comes out on the page. Is it erotic? Well, that's in the crotch of the beholder, isn't it? For those who are into this sort of thing, I'm sure this is a spank bank goldmine. For the rest, I have to say it's written so engagingly it makes me want to try tickle torture no matter how much the thought disturbs me—and that's as far as *this* vanilla bean will go. (Regarding any wider appeal the book may have, the first edition of *Rand* received a vote of confidence when editors Richard Labonté and William J. Mann included the first chapter in the Lambda Award-winning collection *Best Gay Erotica 2005*.)

I recently wrote an essay for *Fever Spores: The Queer Reclamation of William S. Burroughs*, requiring a deep dive into *Queer, Junky*, and, of course, *Naked Lunch*, which I had not revisited in many a year. And as I read *My Name Is Rand*, I was struck more than once by the similarities between *Rand* and *Naked Lunch*. Surely many of the scenes which take place in The Compound, and indeed, The Compound itself is a Dr. Benway episode writ large. The facelessness, the helplessness, the fear, the torture, the otherness—it's all there waiting for both Bill Lee and Rand. The emotional and erotic truth of these books is overwhelming. They take no prisoners. Both state their weirdness parameters at the get-go, then proceed to make good on pushing their respective envelopes of addiction.

But it's time to show rather than tell. Close the curtains and lock your doors. Loosen your belt. Have some water ready, either for drinking or splashing on your face. Paper towels to wipe up any…uh, untoward spills. Depending on your tech level, turn the page or swipe, and begin.

You have nothing to lose that you shouldn't already have lost.

JW
November 2023

ACKNOWLEDGEMENTS

Thanks to Tom Cardamone, Sven Davisson, and Jerry L. Wheeler.

Special thanks to Greg Wharton and Ian Philips of Suspect Thoughts Press, who believed in *My Name Is Rand* since the beginning.

Portions of *My Name Is Rand* have appeared in *Best Gay Erotica 2005* (Richard Labonté and William J. Mann, eds.); *Love Under Foot: An Erotic Celebration of Feet* (Greg Wharton and M. Christian, eds.); and in the webzine *Velvet Mafia* (Sean Meriwether, ed.)

For Ralph, who makes all things possible

I. MY NAME IS RAND

1. GRANGER

It was 3:05 p.m. as I took the turnoff into Granger's neighborhood. To the southeast lay the city, crowded and noisy, but you'd never know it from these quiet streets and small, well-kept homes. Each front yard had one or two trees. The lawns were uniformly clipped, free of fallen leaves or stray toys. They were white houses, mostly, including Granger's, so square and bright in the afternoon sun that it seemed to hover a few feet off the ground.

I pulled into the driveway, turned off my engine and listened to it ticking as it cooled. It had been a long drive across state, with not much to see and a lot to think about. Picturing myself at this very moment, about to meet Granger, ready to discover if I'd been led down the right path. But readiness wasn't something I'd packed in my small bag along with a change of clothes and tape recorder; at the moment it was such a foreign concept that I touched the ignition key, more than halfway inclined to slip into reverse, get away while I still could. Instead I stared at Granger's screen door, and realized in a minute or so that he was standing there, his outline assembling slowly, a tall broad man wearing white, his face a grayish mystery.

I rolled down my window. "Am I okay here," I asked, "or should I park on the street?"

"You're fine." His voice was loud and deep and welcoming, as if I were an old friend or relative. "Come on in."

"Thanks." Always self-critical, I felt a surge of pride, as if I had passed a test: voice normal, nerves normal. It was possible to feel ordinary as I slid out of my small SUV, bag in hand, and approached the door, Granger still a ghost behind the screen.

I set my bag down in the living room, and Granger gave me a tour of the house, which he had just moved into a few weeks earlier. My first really clear look at him was from behind as I followed him down a hallway. He was an ex-Marine, with a short gray crewcut and strong frame, his t-shirt stretched taut across a muscular back and shoulders. His white shorts contrasted well with his tanned furry legs, the kind of legs that could carry a man into and out of all kinds of trouble, legs that would always land a man on his feet. His face, his eyes were still mysteries.

The house was much larger than it looked from the outside. He led me through a generous sun porch down to the basement, which he'd had finished in oak. Half of it had once been a party room, judging by the counter that could easily serve as a bar, and in the other half sat a white washer and dryer. "Also," he said, "I want to build a room over here. For a rack, and some stocks, and a few other things."

"You could have yourself quite a decent torture chamber down here," I said.

"It will come. In time." In the weak light from the basement window Granger's smile, framed by a closely trimmed mustache and beard, was confident. He wore a small gold ring in his left ear. I still wanted a good look at his eyes.

We sat out on the front stoop for a while, facing the sun that had dimmed just perceptibly, nudging the clock toward late afternoon, enriching the lawns and houses with a light more gold than yellow. A few neighbors came and went, some of them waving as they got in or out of their cars. It seemed like a pleasantly integrated neighborhood, a far cry from the redneck suburbs that surrounded the city where I lived.

"It's been years," I said, "since I've seen a neighborhood this quiet."

"It's quiet all the time, too," Granger said. He was wearing sunglasses now. "Even on weekends. No kids on this block."

"And your house is soundproof?"

"Bet your ass." Again that smile, not only confident but anticipating something good.

"Was that the first thing you asked your real estate agent—whether anybody would hear guys screaming in this house?"

Granger laughed. "It wasn't the first thing, but it was high on the list."

I almost asked him then if I could see his eyes. But how do you ask that question? I was working to make every gesture and word project self-assurance, as if I constantly traveled to meet strangers for intimate encounters and this was just one more.

"Let's go inside," he said finally, as the sun came close to touching the tree line.

In the living room I accepted the beer he offered. He had switched on a lamp and as he handed me the beer I got my first good look at his eyes. They were light-colored, a hazel that was almost gray, but their size made up for their paleness—that, and the way they searched my face as if every part of me was to be found there. Eyes that could seek and find anything, with or without cooperation. *Escape proof.* I was close to picking up my bag and retreating while I still could.

"Sit down," he said. "Let's talk."

Like many men I had known, Granger could talk about his erotic history the way others talked about their banking careers or hunting dogs. He took it for granted that I was an expert in homoerotics, had handled male bodies and let them handle me with a familiarity that bred an appetite for more. He assumed I

[3]

had fucked myself raw, sucked cock till my face turned inside out, and jacked off dicks till my palms were callused. It was when he got to our mutual obsession that my heartbeat sped up and my dickhead stirred in my jeans.

He had learned at an early age that he could make other boys helpless by tickling them, and that it was almost unbearably exciting. As he grew up, reducing a boy to breathless laughter and eye-rolling panic became the central ritual of his life. It got him in trouble, the way he single-mindedly pursued his victims; but it also gave him an expertise in stimulation that few others were able to obtain in a lifetime. He explained this to me, not as a braggart but as a man who need make no apologies for what he has diligently earned. He couldn't relate all of his experiences, but he told me enough so that, after a while, my tongue felt dry and swollen, and I realized I'd been sitting and listening to him with my mouth hanging open.

One of the incidents he told me about happened when he was in the service. I had got the facts wrong, he was an ex-Navy man. "We had something called Crossing the Line," he told me. "It was kind of ceremony for the new ensigns who haven't crossed the equator before. First timers. Wogs, we called them. The official part of it took place on deck, where we made them crawl and slide on their ass through a garbage trough, shit like that. But then there was the shit that went on below deck, especially if you had a wog who was cocky or troublesome or on somebody's bad side. That's what happened with this one kid, a Hispanic kid from Austin. He was a pain in the ass, a backtalker and all-around jerk. So us shellbacks gave him an initiation of our own. We tied him naked to his bunk, his feet and wrists knotted nice and tight so he couldn't move. It was the first time I ever saw a guy tied down like that, and I was ready to bust a nut just watching him try to squirm. All we were going to do was cover him in grease, maybe stick the tip of a grease gun up his ass and give him an enema. But I was drawn to those big brown helpless feet, the way he was flexing them, wiggling his toes, it was like they were *talking* to me. We were all standing around him, taunting him, and I reached out for one of those toes and squeezed it. 'This little piggy,' I said, and he surprised the shit out of me—he *howled*, just from having his big toe squeezed.

"I let my fingers play around with his toes some more, and he was just hysterical. You know how guys can pick up on another guy's weakness, it wasn't lost on any of us that this kid was ticklish as hell. Before long all twelve of us were taking turns torturing him, seeing where we could get him the worst. I tended to stay at his feet, he couldn't stand to have them touched. But he was ticklish on his belly and ribs and armpits too—just about everywhere. There wasn't a piece of him that we left alone. By the end of it all twelve of us were on him, making him scream to wake the dead. Can you imagine that, twenty-four hands on you, all at the same time? He pissed the bed and ended up crying like a baby. We fucked him up *bad*."

As he talked I watched his eyes, those all-encompassing eyes, and was somehow unaware that he'd moved from his chair onto the sofa beside me until his hand brushed my arm and I jumped. I was everything he wanted, everything that excited him; and the more I realized it the more I shrank away, as if I could retract my ticklish nerve-ends the way a turtle hides in its shell. I was certain that I couldn't stand to be touched, not by him, not anywhere.

"Down at the end of that hall," he said. "Get going."

I sat and blinked at him. If just one of his large groping fingers touched my naked skin, I'd die.

"I said *move!*"

The bedroom had light green walls, small shaded lamps, and a double bed with an immaculate white spread. It was the kind of room you'd find in a B&B, comfortable and inviting—not threatening in the least. But my knees shook as I looked around, because the harmlessness of the setting seemed to *add* something threatening to it.

Granger grabbed the center of the bedspread with his fist, snatched it off the bed, rolled it up in a ball, and tossed it in a corner. From a drawer he took some cloth restraints—surgical restraints, he said, the kind they used in hospitals. He didn't look directly at me as he spoke, it was as if he were speaking aloud to his obsession, stoking it with words. "Some tools," he said, taking a box from a chest of drawers. I saw hairbrushes, regular and electric toothbrushes, feathers, some wicked-looking hair picks, thick pipe cleaners. I reached out to touch one of the brushes, one he had told me about the first time we chatted online. Called "the widowmaker," it had steel bristles with rounded nylon tips, and was deadly on the soles of the feet.

He was getting out yet another bag of tools when the doorbell rang. He left to answer it. I was having trouble getting my excited breathing under control. I paced in the narrow space between the bed and the shuttered window, then moved out into the hall. Granger stood at the front door, talking to someone—a solicitor?—standing outside on the stoop. While they chatted I could barely take my eyes off Granger's left hand. It was in constant motion, the fingers stiffening, then springing into claws, then wriggling ferociously—tickling, tickling the air. Was it a signal to me, or did that hand really have a mind of its own, independent from the judgment and will that normally made it run?

***

I lay naked on the cool sheet, my head propped up enough so I could watch Granger peel off his shirt and shorts in a couple of neat stripper moves. His dick—the kind of dick that can stop an argument—preceded the rest of him from then on, bobbing and swaying as he performed his bondage chores. He grabbed my ankles and easily pulled me down toward the bottom edge of the bed, where he tied my ankles together, first wrapping them in a towel so the black cord wouldn't cut into the skin. A second length of cord led from my bound ankles to a fixture on the floor at the foot of the bed. Next he slid toe-rings over my big toes, metal rings that tickled as he fitted them snug, making me gasp. It wasn't a good sign: if my toes were that ticklish, what kind of chance did I have? He tied cords leading from the rings to the cords securing my ankles, so I now had feet that couldn't move up or down or side to side, soles that couldn't flex, toes that couldn't clench. By the time he had fastened the wrist restraints, stretching my arms to the limit, and blindfolded me with a tight dark cloth, I knew the utter helplessness of a victim, unable to fend off the merest threat.

He showed me how easy it was for him, reducing me to blind laughter within a matter of seconds—playfully, using a big soft feather on my nostrils, violating my nose, shoving tickling sensations up into my brain till I was begging him to stop. From there it was a short trip to my ears, feathering all in and around them as I felt them grow, my ticklish ears becoming all of me, then expanding into the room, the street, the city. The tickler and his feathers grew, too, keeping in step with sensation as my laughter, already hoarse, swallowed up all other sound.

I was half out of my mind, and so far he had only touched my nose and ears. He had a lot to teach me just by moving as far down as my neck, where the feathers had me giggling and sputtering like a child, twisting my head, exposing new spots, new angles to the torture. Now my body was a map of the known and the unknown, and I gasped as he reached each frontier, my shoulders, my upper chest….

When he reached my armpits I began to beg in earnest. His strong, quick fingers whirred like eggbeaters in those tender pockets, and I was twisting my head again, choking out laughter that rose in pitch and volume, then babbling whenever my breath could find room, an automatic string of *stop-it-please-stop-it* and *don't-do-it-don't-do-it*….

Then he jumped whole continents, moving from my armpits to my feet, and I realized how much power he had, how he could turn me into anything. His strong fingers raked my soles over and over, and it was as if it had been ordained long ago that these were the fingers that could tickle me to death. He paused only to soften up my feet with baby oil and slicken them with lotion. Then he took up the deadly brush—the widowmaker—and ground its stiff bristles into my arches. My head exploded. I screamed at him, said I was going to die if he didn't stop. I spent my precious breath begging him, using every dirty promise, every filthy bribe I could think of, pledging to be his dick-slave, to jack him off, suck his cock, lick his balls, massage his prostate if only he'd stop tickling me. I promised him everything I could think of short of letting him fuck me in the ass, which I'd never let a man do during a first encounter. But my mouth could serve him, I swore I'd make him come like he'd never come before, honest to Christ, he'd never be sorry he took mercy on me….

"*Mercy?*" He laughed like hell as he scrubbed the flesh beneath my tightly stretched toes. When he finally paused just long enough to say, "Now I think I'm gonna work *between* your toes for a while," I could picture what he was doing, taking up a

[8]

handful of the thick pipe cleaners.

Much later, when I was finally free and had had a chance to recover, and we were sitting on the red sofa in his living room, he called me on those promises. I pointed out that those promises had been pleas for a mercy I'd never received. His counter-argument was convincing, though: "You better get to work, or the next session will be even worse."

To make his point he grabbed my feet and used his fingernails on my soles. That flipped a switch and I was instantly helpless, writhing and sputtering about how good I could make his dick feel.

"So do it," he said.

I sank to the floor, took his dick in my mouth and, excited by the feel of his dickhead against my palate, sucked as if my life depended on it, which it probably did. I sucked and jacked his dick, licked his glistening balls, soaked his groin and navel with my tongue. He lay back, his eyes closed, moaning quite seriously. I sucked his achingly hard dick again till he was at the point of coming, then moved back to his balls. His moans were louder than ever. I spread his thighs wider, the more easily to reach down and manipulate his prostate with my fingertips. Unable to resist his hairy thighs, I let my fingers roam there too, stroking, then lightly squeezing. His moans grew shorter, sharper. As I continued working his dick with my mouth I let two fingers explore between his cheeks to find his asshole, prying and rubbing and rimming it.

When he was close to coming I started jacking his dick for all I was worth. His dickhead popped free from my mouth and he came in an explosion so long and hard that it left me sitting against the wall with my face, neck, and chest soaked with cum. I was so fucking wet, I thought his dick had literally blown up.

Then I got in his face. He seemed barely conscious, moaning and shaking his head in disbelief at what I'd made him feel. But I knew he was hearing me as I said to him, "Now here is what I want you to do. Tie me up and tickle me, and keep it steady. Don't stop for a second, till you've tickled me out of my mind. Make me your slave."

In no time I was tightly stretched, tied down and blindfolded again. I knew whatever he had done to me before was now going to be ten times worse, but it turned out I was wrong. It was a hundred times worse. His tickling was relentless, keeping me in such steady laughter that I couldn't speak. Even when he stopped to lotion up my feet for the widowmaker, I couldn't beg for mercy because I was panting so hard. Those bristles ground into my soles again and I was screaming, a steady hoarsening wail that rose in pitch and intensity like a siren gone haywire, taking all my breath, threatening to burst my own eardrums. I screamed for what seemed like forever as he scrubbed my slickened feet all over with those bristles, and I was no longer tied to a bed but floating, suspended in endless space, held aloft by nothing but agony.

When that particular torture was over I had no time to recover, for he was at the rest of me again, from my neck to my knees, and my screams subsided into steady, hysterical laughter as his strong, quick fingers seemed to move everywhere at once. When I could get out a word, finally, one exhausted word, it was "Don't!"

"Don't what?" he asked. "Don't what?" But of course he wouldn't stop long enough to let me get out another word, I was off on another course of breathless laughter.

"Don't!" I managed to say again, perhaps an hour later.

"Don't what?" he asked again, jabbing my belly with all

ten fingers, my laughter so shrill now that it sounded like the keening of a madman throwing himself against the rubber walls of his cell.

When the widowmaker came again I broke completely. The time when I thought he *couldn't* totally break me belonged to ancient history, when the earth was flat. Now, with those bristles as merciless as fire on the center of my soles and beneath my toes, I knew, for the first time, what it was like to lose the will to survive. Through my struggling the cords had loosened enough so I could clench my toes a bit; but now, after another long, high-pitched wail, I relaxed them for the first time, allowing them to spread, *surrendering* them to him. Immediately bristles forced themselves where they couldn't quite reach before. I was laughing, babbling, and wailing all at the same time.

After my feet had been totally destroyed, broken down into ticklish molecules and down again into nothing, he moved back to the rest of me, kneading, squeezing, pitilessly poking and pulling the lethally sensitized flesh from my neck to my thighs. I was reduced to panting with my tongue hanging out, drooling down my chin like an idiot.

The session lasted all night.

***

The next day, after we'd slept a few hours—I'd stayed on the bed, too weak to move from the sweat-soaked sheet—we had eggs and toast, sitting naked at the kitchen table with a pot of black coffee, then ended up on the red sofa again. I lay on my belly with my feet hooked over his thigh, which let him play with my soles with his right hand as he jacked himself off with his left. After a while he said, "Now I want your ribs," and like the obedient tickle-slave I'd become I rolled over, got to my knees, and raised my arms above my head. The unspoken rules of engagement demanded that, if I wanted to get him to stop tickling my ribs, I had to beg him to tickle my belly; and in order to rescue my poor sore belly I had to beg him to tickle my armpits. "Please, master," I said again and again, offering up my feet, then my lower back. Soon we were writhing together, slick with sweat and precum, and I had his dick in my mouth. It seemed even bigger today, as if it had swollen with use. He had to admit that he liked my dick too, showing it in his own way: no obliging hand jobs or sweet suckoffs, not without a lot of agonizing apple-polishing first. Did it make me more ticklish? Of course it did. Everything did—breathing the air, processing oxygen, replacing dead cells with new ones.

Sometime in the afternoon we got stoned. I was afraid at first, but fear had also become as standard as breathing. Being with Granger was all about fear, because I was so scared of being tickled to death and he was so ready to make it happen. The grass that we smoked was moist, as if he grew it himself in the backyard. Maybe he did; a hidden plot of marijuana was no more subversive than a torture chamber, which he did a pretty good job of improvising even if he didn't have all the equipment yet.

Being stoned *was* dangerous. My buzzing brain kept losing track of my skin. There I was with my feet in his face, shoving them against his tongue and teeth; how'd *that* happen? And how did I ever allow him to wrap me in plastic like a mummy? Not that it was much work for him—he had only to spread the thick plastic sheet on the floor, have me lie down on it, grab an edge and roll. His work consisted of tying ropes to keep the plastic in place, making absolutely sure I couldn't move my arms, hands, or even fingers. As I lay on my back, completely helpless, he put toe-rings on my feet and secured them. I was breathing hard, out of panic. This was an advanced stage of bondage, much different from being tied spread-eagle to a bed, where it was at least possible to move enough to prove to yourself you were still alive. The only part of my body I could move at all was my head, and that not very much. It didn't seem to count, anyway, when there was little my head could do but measure the devastation to come, like a seismograph.

"Granger?" I asked, just wanting to hear his voice. "Hey, Granger." He wasn't near my stretched, bound feet; where was he? Twisting my head to the left, I could glimpse the kitchen area, the light from the open refrigerator glowing on the tiles. Cellophane crackled, a jar popped its lid. The son of a bitch was making himself a sandwich. Pulling a chair over to the kitchen counter, he sat where I could see his bare feet as he ate, making plenty of slurping and smacking sounds but not saying a word. "Hey, Granger." He was probably reading a magazine, too. "Granger, goddamn it!"

It was tough to appraise a situation where, thanks to pot, my senses lagged behind my observations. I was in deep trouble, its depth revealing itself slowly, like layers of a dream. While most of me could do nothing, my pot-sensitized feet perked up like a retriever's ears, registering everything—air currents, particles of dust, sound waves from Granger's squeaking chair. Idiot feet, bragging about how sensitive they were, as if to reassure me. "Hey, Granger?" I said. Maybe it wasn't too late to call this off. "Granger." I was growing warm in my plastic cocoon, my sweat seeming to tighten the sheath even more. "Granger," I said, twisting my head toward his bare feet on the kitchen floor, all I could see of him. Unlike mine, his feet were confident, in control. Feet that would always land a man on his legs. What, what was

I going to do? *What could I do?* The unacceptable *nothing* echoed through my mind in a voice very much like Granger's. I shook my head vigorously, like a child throwing a tantrum, until I heard Granger's voice again, for real this time.

"Here you go," he said. As if he were handing me a glass of water, instead of fitting a blindfold over my eyes. "Here you go," and there I went, into total darkness.

What he did to my feet over the next hour should not have been done to anyone, ever. I would never know what he used on them, for he refused to tell me, even after he finally stopped. I assumed it was something from his kitchen, something that was never meant to be used on human flesh. It burrowed into the core of my ticklishness and multiplied like a corrosive virus, flaying my feet down to raw nerves. At each touch I howled a desperate laughter and the touching never stopped; he kept me on the brink of passing out but I never quite crossed over. When he finally stopped tickling me I kept howling, stuck in my hysteria till he grabbed my chin with one hand, turned my head back and forth. It was then I knew it was over, also realizing that my midsection had become unbearably warm and moist: I had pissed myself.

***

Something was different in me after that. For a long time I sat across the living room from Granger and looked at him looking at me. He sat with one bare leg hiked up, a forearm resting on his knee, a vaguely satisfied expression on his face, the look of a champion trying to appear humble. Even his dick, which I had rubbed and sucked raw over the past twenty-four hours, looked satisfied, lying on his belly as if it were taking a well-deserved nap. Still half-stoned and hardly sane, I began listening, almost against my will, to the tiny voice in that part of my brain that could still organize thought. The voice was telling me that somehow I was going to have to pull myself together. Somewhere the world kept turning, and I would have to join it again.

"You want anything to eat?" Granger asked.

I shook my head.

"Anything to drink? Water?"

I just looked at him. "How am I going to do this?" I asked.

"Don't worry," he said. "Just take it slow. Do you want to make a phone call?"

Yes, that was another thing that just came back to me: I was not going to be able to make it all the way across the state tonight as I had originally planned. I needed at least another couple of hours before I would be in any shape to drive. I looked at my watch and figured out, with the time-consuming, roundabout logic of someone under the influence of too much stimulation, that David would not be home from his law office yet, even though it was Saturday. That meant I would get his answering machine. That was okay, I could handle being coherent enough to leave a message.

I got my long-distance calling card from my wallet and said to Granger, "I'll be right back." I used the phone in the bedroom, and again I was struck by how innocuous it looked, the bed neatly made, the spread back in place, the restraints and tickling tools hidden away. The curtains were open, the room glowing in the fading light of early evening.

As I had expected, after four rings the answering machine picked up. What I didn't expect was that David had changed his outgoing message. Instead of announcing rather formally that he couldn't come to the phone, he said only, "Hi, I'm not home right now. You know what to do." The beep followed immediately, but it took me a few more seconds to collect my wits.

I'd always heard that when you were dying your whole life flashed before your eyes. Sitting on the edge of Granger's bed with the receiver in my hand, I must have experienced a kind of small death, during which my relationship with David, just a recent part of my life, played out before me like a videotape on fast-forward. During the year we'd known each other we'd had some incredible sex, and many other intensely enjoyable moments; but there had also been that evening, over candlelight and wine, when I had told David that I loved him. He didn't know, couldn't have known, how much it had cost me to say that, how much courage it took, how it filled me with both liberation and fear to say those words. As soon as they were out of my mouth I began to tremble, and my eyes slowly filled with tears as I watched David's face.

"Thank you, Rand," he said, as if I were a client who had just signed a contract. He went on to explain that, while he was moved by my sentiment, he did not feel that he was truly capable of loving anyone other than himself—never had been, never would be. His smile was kind, but just slightly condescending, as if I had made an error in judgment that could have been avoided if only I'd been a bit smarter.

After that night our relationship continued as before—on the surface, at least. But neither of us could deny that things had changed. We were like two people in an earthquake, assuring each other that all was well even as we scrambled to try to keep our balance. So it was with only a small sense of betrayal that I had sought contact with another man—Granger—and that I could leave David a message that, while not untruthful, hardly hinted at what I had been through over the last couple of days.

"Listen," I said to his machine, "I'm not going to make it home this evening after all. I haven't started out yet. I'll just drive for a couple of hours tonight and make the rest of the trip tomorrow morning. I'll call you when I get home." I hoped that my voice sounded calm, non-stoned, and upbeat—the very opposite of how I felt. Guilt was dragging me down, not because of what I had done but because of what it had meant to me. Even David's voice on the answering machine had depressed me—that snappy, self-assured "You know what to do." Instead of my carefully worded message I could have said, "No, David, I don't know what to do. Return to our hopeless relationship? If that's what I need to do, then why do I *want*…something else? What do you do when you want something else, when you've been driven over the edge and there's no turning back?"

***

By my watch it was 8:15 when I left. Granger, still naked, saw me to the door. Even in the hallway the air reeked of sweat and cum and piss, and I felt I had his scent on me too—hard to describe, a clean but strong smell, like a no-nonsense soap. In spite of what they had done to me I was going to miss his enormous hands. And his dick, which I stooped down and took in my mouth one last time, clutching it with my tongue. He cuffed me on the shoulder as I picked up my bag and stepped outside. The evening sun was surprisingly strong.

I was still feeling a little stoned, and drove with the kind of overcompensation that can be so amusing in someone who's high—keeping twenty miles under the speed limit, braking far in advance of a red light. There wasn't much traffic, though, on the quiet streets leading to the highway.

The interstate was a different matter, especially at the point where it merged with another major highway. Suddenly I found myself in the midst of eight lanes of stalled traffic—a thousand taillights flaring at random as brakes were lightly touched, no car moving more than a few inches at a time. Whatever caused the jam lay far ahead, unseen; I couldn't spot even the flashing lights of a police car or ambulance. I was headed in the right direction, but was I in the correct lane? The more I thought about it, the more it seemed I should move one lane to the left, to avoid being forced onto an exit I didn't want to take. Hoping for the best, I switched on my blinker. There was no break in the solid line of cars I wanted to merge with, but in less than a minute, as the traffic crawled forward, a gap appeared. I eased into it, waving "Thanks!" to the driver who was now behind me.

Now I noticed that many cars were changing lanes. Other drivers like me were worried about suddenly finding themselves on an exit ramp they didn't want, while those toward the center of the merged highways were no doubt eyeing the lanes to their right and left and thinking, *Hmm, they seem to be moving just a little bit faster*…. By itself this wasn't surprising; what astonished me was how easily each transition occurred, with no impatience, no honking of horns. Cars moved as easily to the left and right as if all were planned, choreographed like a crowd scene where individual actions look random yet form a coherent whole when seen from a distance. The participants moved steadily and considerately, trusting that, with no more contact among us than flashing turn signals, we all knew what to do.

It seemed like a long time before traffic moved freely again. The ugly, overfamiliar highway offered little to see but gently rolling countryside, flat and featureless. I kept to the speed limit, letting tractor-trailers and anxious SUVs rush by on my left. Alert now, I could see each step of the journey ahead: stopping at a cheap but adequate motel, catching seven or eight hours' sleep and taking off again with a thermos full of coffee, finally reaching home around noon. Calling David, who would surely be at home then, reading the Sunday paper. I'd told him that I was visiting an "old friend." He'd have no inkling of what I'd been through; if I tried to explain that I had been tied up and tickled to within an inch of my life he would only stare at me, wide-eyed and openmouthed, letting his *Parade* magazine fall to the floor.

Traffic grew sparse as I approached the center of the state. With no oncoming headlights or a clear radio station to keep me company, I reached into my bag on the passenger's seat and found the cassette tape player. Granger had turned it on and kept it near me during our most intense sessions. As soon as I pressed the PLAY button my own raucous laughter, so sharp and clear in the dark of night, took my breath away. I was neither seeing him nor feeling him, but at that moment Granger seemed more alive than anyone I had ever known.

***

The tape was still playing when I pulled off the road. Rest areas were few, and I felt an urgency that couldn't wait another sixty miles. A sign pointed to the left for trucks, right for cars. I turned right and pulled into the nearly empty lot. The rest rooms were in a brick building designed to look like a small cottage, complete with white shutters on the windows, white doors with brass knobs. I sat in my car listening to my own breathless, desperate laughter as a man came out the door nearest me. Then another man came out. The two headed toward separate cars near the end of the lot, their steps careful, their windbreakers zipped up. They had just jacked or sucked each other off or maybe even fucked in the men's room. It was such an old story that I was surprised it still went on. For a Saturday night, though, there were not many cars around. Clearly this wasn't a central cruising spot but a remote outpost.

I closed my eyes for a second. When I opened them again I felt warm, almost feverish. Sweat had collected under my arms, between my legs—the by-product of an overheated, unexpected sleep. I opened my window and sat with the slightly cool air drifting over me. In my rearview mirror a blue panel truck passed by slowly, the driver, a brute with a shaved head, staring at me— or was he? I watched the truck move slowly down the line of cars. I looked at my watch: 10:05.

I left the car and looked to see what had happened to the blue truck. It had parked farther down the lot, out of sight. Had the driver really looked at me, and if so, why? Was he looking for a trick, or a mugging victim? A wave of melancholy swept over me as I saw how quickly I was adapting to everyday life again—the trepidation, the paranoia that got applied each day like underarm deodorant. *It's true*, this paranoia told me, *you have to be careful in a place like this. Nobody knows exactly where you are, after all. You could disappear, your car could be dealt with, you'd never be heard from again.*

I whistled a tune as I crossed the short lawn with the cassette player in hand. *You'd never be heard from again* was not, in the end, as persuasive as the memory of how I sounded on tape. I wasn't ready, anyway, to leave the stepped-up reality of erotic adventure. Next to the cottage I stopped at the bank of vending machines behind theft-proof bars and bought myself a bottle of iced tea. Not wanting to take it into the men's room with me, I placed it on the walk next to a concrete cigarette urn. It was a safekeeper, a sign that I would return.

No one else was in the men's room. There were two urinals and three toilet stalls. I used a urinal, then washed my face and hands, taking my time. Did I treasure the solitude and quiet, or did I *want* someone to appear? Something kept me standing before the polished metal mirror long after I'd combed my hair. Finally I walked, with a distinct sense of unreality, past the toilet stalls and stepped into the last one, a handicapped stall that seemed larger than my bedroom. Without dropping my pants I sat on the toilet. It was so quiet. Somewhere across the wooded lot huge trucks were pulling in or leaving, but I couldn't hear a sound.

The floor was gray slate. I reached down and untied the lace of my right sneaker. For a long time I sat and looked at that unlaced sneaker, so white against the floor that looked…so cold. Finally I slid that sneaker off, and the white crew sock. Then I let my foot drop, and the feel of that cold slate against my sole, so recently tenderized by extreme tickling, brought a groan from deep in my gut. The groan became a moan, a helpless, begging sound. The cold floor was torturing my poor ticklish skin and there was nothing I could do, it was as if my foot were held fast by cruel hands that would tickle it forever.

Through half-closed eyes I looked at the tape player in my hand, pressed the PLAY button. Instantly laughter filled the room—exhausted, hysterical laughter echoing off the walls. Then there were words—I couldn't remember speaking them but there they were. It was after Granger had broken me, and I was screaming at him. I rewound the tape and listened again, making sense of it this time. *Go ahead and tickle me to death,* I screamed, *I don't care anymore! Do your worst, you bastard!* Then more of that mad, driving laughter.

As loud as the tape was, it couldn't disguise another sound— the low, stuttering creak of the rest room door opening. I heard, just faintly under the noise of my recorded screaming, the scuff of a footstep, then another. This unseen man...was he scared by the insane laughter echoing off the walls? Or was he *curious*?

I kept the tape playing, kept my bare foot flat against the tickling floor as I watched the space under the stall door. In a moment two orange work boots stepped carefully into view. They were uncertain, those boots, they couldn't quite stay still as my screams and laughter echoed from the small black box.

"Jesus," said the man outside the stall. I held my breath and heard nothing more than my own recorded laughter. I turned it off, just long enough to rewind it. When I turned it back on, the words were there: *Go ahead and tickle me to death, I don't care anymore!*

"Hey! You all right in there?"

I let the tape run. The latch on the stall door had barely caught, it wouldn't take much pressure to open it.

"Hey! What's goin' on?"

The work boots came closer. Four fingers appeared over the top of the stall door, and it swung outward with barely a hitch.

The man who stood facing me had a shaved head, a reddish mustache and goatee, and a broad, muscular frame. I recognized him as the young man with the blue panel truck. He shook his head, said "What the hell...?"

I turned off the tape player. "That was me," I said. My knees were trembling, like my voice. "That was me getting tickled. Just like now...this floor...it's tickling my foot."

The man rubbed his mouth with the back of his hand. His sparse mustache was not disturbed by the gesture. He didn't seem to know where to look, at me or at the walls where my laughter had echoed a few seconds earlier. "Jesus Christ," he said.

I stayed perfectly still, watching him.

He looked down at the floor, then at me. His hands were on his hips. One boot tapped against the floor, slowly. Finally he sank to his knees, very suddenly, and before I could move or speak he placed his hand on my left sneaker.

I gasped.

With his other hand he untied the sneaker. Then he used both hands to take it off. This left my white sock, which he peeled away slowly. Then he grabbed my ankle and slapped my bare foot against the floor.

I howled. I thought I might faint, or perhaps had fainted, but when I opened my eyes he was still crouching before me, looking me straight in the eye. He nodded, once, then stood up.

"Come on," he said.

I grabbed the tape player with a trembling hand and stood up, my feet nearly crying out as my full weight pressed them to that cold floor. I looked around for my socks and sneakers and saw that he held them, the sneakers swinging from his right hand with the socks balled up in them. He swung them toward me, just a bit, then pulled them back, as if to say I wouldn't need them anymore.

"Come on," he said again.

I followed him across the cold floor and outside, to the cement sidewalk. He had an agitated walk, his heels hitting the cement a little too hard. We passed my car, and for a split second I felt I was going to say something or make a sound to indicate that it was my car we were passing. Then I felt an incredible relief that I had kept the secret. And *then* I remembered that he had seen me sitting in my car, I was sure he had. Hell, he could have followed me here all the way from Granger's, for all I knew. Or—how about this?—he could be a cop, ready to charge me with something.

That was wishful thinking.

He left the sidewalk, crossing the grass toward the far end of the lot. I stopped. He must have sensed I wasn't following him anymore, for he turned around.

"I can't walk on the grass," I said. "My feet…."

"Come on," he said a third time.

"Please. Please don't make me do this."

He turned away and kept walking.

Very carefully, I stepped onto the grass. It wasn't as cold as the slate floor but it was just as cruel, its blades poking at my soles even as I stood perfectly still. "I can't…." I watched him walk on ahead of me, and knew I *had* to follow. I decided to take large steps, as large as I could, to get across the lawn as quickly as possible. After a few of these steps I found myself laughing, a few chuckles stirring deep in my throat. Another step, and another, and I was nearly out of breath.

Yes, it was the blue truck that he took me to. I wondered where he had got the nerve to park it here, among the cars, instead of in the truck lot on the other side of the rest area. But then this wasn't a tractor trailer, just a panel truck of the sort that might be used on a farm—for hauling bales of hay, maybe, or even animals.

"Get in," he said.

He started the engine before I reached the passenger's side. If I hesitated too long he might leave without me. I stared at the chrome door handle, just visible in the darkness, and could not quite make my hand reach for it, could not picture myself getting in. Surely this man, who was no more a cop than I was—this angry-looking, muscular young man with his truck that smelled faintly of hay and earth—would drive off without me. It seemed more likely to happen the longer I stood there without raising my hand. He didn't flash his lights, sound his horn, or make a move toward my side of the car.

Goodbye, I thought. *Just pull away.*

That was what was supposed to happen, but it didn't. Instead my hand appeared, all on its own, and lifted the door handle. My hand had made the decision for me, and now I had no choice but to follow.

He didn't even glance at me as I climbed in and sat heavily on the worn springs of the long front seat. When I slammed the door it made a sharp, conclusive sound. I set my feet on the floor and regretted it instantly, for the rubber mat was dirty, covered with things that scraped, scratched, and dug into my soles: grains of sand, tiny pebbles, sharp specks of gravel. I yelled, jerking my feet upward, placing them on the seat between us. My heart sank deep into the pit of my ticklish belly as he turned his head toward me. I couldn't see his eyes but I could *feel* him staring at my feet, the tender soles embedded with grains of dirt and rock.

After what seemed like several minutes he finally spoke. "We're going to be driving for a while, out into the country," he said. "And you're going to be nice and well behaved. Or else." He grabbed my ankles, easily binding them in the grip of one strong hand, and with his other hand he raked the soles of my feet. Again I yelled—I think it was *Help, help!* that time, for what good it did me—but in just a few seconds I couldn't yell or even talk for laughing, laughing breathlessly, desperately as he worked at the soles of my feet, clawing free the dirt and pebbles and leaving the sting of his strong relentless fingers.

"Oh, this is easy," he said. "You make it *so* easy."

Weakened by laughter, trapped by my own hysteria, I could only roll from side to side on the seat, my hands flapping uselessly like the wings of a flightless bird. Insofar as I was able to think, I thought of how unlikely it would be for this man to turn out to be as ruthless and sadistic as, say, Granger. After all, we had met by chance. It *had* to be chance. Probably he had never tickled a man's feet like this before, and he would tire of it quickly and let me go. It was the kind of desperate thought that couldn't last much longer than a soap bubble in the increasingly chilly night air.

"You're not the first ticklish guy I've picked up in this rest area," he said. "You're the most brazen, though. And oh, my friend, you'll suffer for it." He turned on the lights and revved the old, powerful engine. "You'll *suffer*."

He drove down the narrow access ramp to the highway. We didn't stay on the highway for very long, though. I should have been watching, should have noted which exit he took, but I couldn't take my eyes off his profile or the way he sat, his back barely touching the seat. I only knew that at some point we turned off the interstate onto a road that was rough, hilly, and full of twists. By the time I raised myself to see where we were going the road had leveled out, and we were passing small frame houses spaced so widely apart that there must have been crops planted between them, though I couldn't see or smell anything of them in the night. The road still felt rough but it looked smooth in the glow of the headlights, and I understood it was the truck's worn shocks that were giving us a bumpy ride.

The man had not spoken to me again nor, as far as I could tell, even glanced at me. So he startled me when he turned his head and said, "Turn that thing on."

I didn't have to ask what he meant. I found the tape player where it had fallen to the floor and pressed the PLAY button. The recording picked up where it had left off, in the middle of a series of short, sharp screams I had made while Granger attacked my ribs. Because the truck's windows were open and the truck was moving very fast I had to turn the volume up so that my laughing, screaming, and begging could be clearly heard.

Oh please man don't...

Oh Jesus Christ don't touch me there...

You don't want to do that, no!

Please don't tickle my ribs...not like that...you know I can't stand it...

Not like that, you know I can't stand it meant that Granger was lotioning up my feet in preparation for the widowmaker. Soon my voice escalated to a piercing scream and a series of outbursts that sounded more like barking than laughing as he twisted those deadly bristles against the tautly stretched soles of my feet.

Meanwhile we drove faster and faster, the farmhouses more widely spaced now, some set so far back from the road that I could only see a dim light burning here and there.

By the time the young man turned right onto a dirt road we had listened to Granger assaulting my ribs, armpits, sides, and navel, and were heading toward another one-minute stint with the widowmaker. I was begging desperately, breathlessly for Granger to leave my feet alone when the truck lights shone against a gray weathered building and we came to a stop. The lights went out, the engine died. I turned the tape player off and we sat till my ears grew accustomed to the silence and I could make out, barely, the low humming and buzzing and chirping of insects.

What I saw of the house was sparsely furnished, and the room that he took me to had no furniture at all, not even curtains or blinds on its two large windows. It was brightly lit by one bare bulb hanging from the ceiling. "Sit down," he said, and since there was nothing to sit on I lowered myself carefully to the hardwood floor. For a minute or two he paced back and forth across the room, rubbing the back of his head with one hand.

He hardly glanced at me, he was thinking so hard. A couple of times he seemed about to speak, then changed his mind, turning whatever left his lips into a sigh or sputter. I still held the tape player, which had become like a permanent attachment to my hand, and I fingered the PLAY button, wondering if I should turn it on. I was afraid to, because the echoing in this empty room would probably be unbearable. I was also afraid not to, because the silence, broken only by the young man's sputtering and sighing, was also becoming unbearable. Finally I turned the machine on, but adjusted the volume with my thumb so the recording played low, like a TV in an adjoining room. My hysterical laughter continued softly in the background as the young man finally began to speak.

He said his name was Michael. The story he told me was amazing, with levels of detail that sank into my consciousness as he related it several times, with minor variations, over whatever length of time he kept me in that house. I came to know his story as well as I knew my own.

2. MICHAEL

Michael had lived his whole life in the country—not the country as city people imagined it, with rolling hills, lush greenery, and pleasant views in all directions, but the country of the poor, where land lay flat and fallow, where old farmhouses needed paint and were never warm enough in the winter. It was the country of front yard poverty, junk cars and gravel roads and failing general stores. It was the country where snow was too deep in December and sunlight too thin in August, spread across the sky like a layer of margarine. It was the country of not much to do and little to think about.

He spent his teenage years in the home of his uncle and aunt and two older, male cousins. He had come to live with them because his parents had split up and neither of them could afford to keep him. It didn't matter that much to him at the time, and though he didn't know these relatives well he thought he might enjoy living with the other boys. It might be like having brothers.

Uncle Dred's house stood on many acres of land that had not been farmed in a long time. He was a traveling salesman dealing in farm equipment, his territory covering four huge states, and he spent most of his life on the road. Aunt Helen worked as a secretary in a real estate office thirty miles away; she drove off in the morning before the boys left for school and didn't get home until hours after they did.

The Greyhound bus dropped Michael off at his new home on a Sunday early in September. He had only seen these relatives once before, at a funeral—the funeral of Michael's dad's other brother, Uncle Carl. Michael couldn't even name the town now, but more family members than he'd ever seen before had assembled there, in an old brick funeral home that was stifling in July. There was Uncle Dred and Aunt Helen, and their two boys, Jason and Josh; when Michael saw them he thought they were identical twins because they looked so much alike in their starched white shirts and dark suits. Like everyone else at the funeral the boys had mumbled a lot and mostly stared at the floor. So Michael was really seeing them for the first time on this Sunday, seeing that they did not look just alike after all, at least not anymore: they dressed the same, in corduroys worn at the knees and faded plaid shirts, but Jason was the handsomer one, with piercing blue eyes and the kind of profile you'd see on an Army recruitment poster. He laughed often, and his laugh was loud: haw-*haw*. Josh's face was softer, his chin weaker, but he seemed more thoughtful, smarter than his brother.

That Sunday was a day of organized boredom, the boys helping Aunt Helen—Uncle Dred was on the road—with work around the house and yard, the boys moving quickly, dully, not saying much. Then a Sunday dinner of pork roast and boiled potatoes and too much gravy.

At bedtime Michael learned that he and his cousins would be sharing a bedroom. In a house that big, it seemed strange. It was even stranger when they undressed for the night. With all three of them in the bedroom and the door closed, the older boys stripped off their clothes slowly, deliberately, staring at Michael all the time. Michael tried to look away without seeming awkward, as if older boys undressed in front of him all the time. In fact he had rarely seen other boys undressed and was totally unprepared for the sight of his naked cousins. They had muscular builds, and hair on their chests, legs, and arms. Their hands were large and as they stood looking at Michael their fingers seemed to twitch excitedly. They stood close to each other, their hips nearly touching, their man-sized cocks half-erect, and stared at Michael as he pulled off his briefs, getting naked because his cousins were naked. Then he turned away and made himself busy folding his jeans. He was intensely aware of himself—a skinny fourteen-year-old with a crewcut, a big Adam's apple, and a partial hard-on, the male energy in the room making his dick too curious to keep its head down. Then Josh snapped off the light and they were in their separate beds, Michael keenly aware of the warm flesh and male scents surrounding him. He wanted to touch himself but didn't quite dare with the other boys so close, making him toss and turn and pray restlessly for sleep.

**

The two cousins lost no time in telling their new sibling what he could expect from them. In fact, they didn't tell him, they showed him, on that first Monday after school.

They were going to play a game, they said, and took Michael up to the second floor of the farmhouse, to one of the rooms that weren't used for anything. Michael wondered what they could possibly do in an empty room. As soon as they were inside, the older boys stood between him and the door, their hands at their sides.

Michael's head was still swimming from his first day at the huge regional high school, where he was a freshman, Josh a junior, and Jason a senior. It was a chilly place with white classrooms and tinted windows and more kids than Michael had ever seen. He had moved through a day of no familiar sights, sounds, or smells, and then had found his cousins out in back of the school smoking cigarettes and using cusswords he'd never heard before. Now that he was alone in the house with them, with his uncle away and his aunt not due home for hours, they were staring at him as they had the night before, their fingers twitching with excitement. In his mind the worst possible case took form: they wanted to smack him around to show how tough they were. He smiled, hoping it was a tough kind of smile, the smile of a kid who just didn't care. "So what's going on?" he asked.

The expression on Jason's face was dead serious. His hands clenched into fists again and again as he shifted his weight from one foot to the other. "Nothing," he said.

Michael backed up a few steps across the bare wood floor. There was a window behind him, but it was too high to jump from.

"We're just going to find out if you're ticklish," Jason said.

Michael wasn't sure what to make of this. He had never really been tickled, except maybe briefly by his father. "Sounds like kind of a dumb game," he said, though he tried to keep his half-smile as he said it. He was a little relieved that they weren't going to beat him up—unless by "ticklish" they meant something else, something that would hurt. Obviously they were going to *touch* him in some way, and again his face reddened, because the night before when they were all naked he had wished that his cousins would touch him. The yearning was there, the undeniable longing that he dared not think too much about. Now he stood very still and waited, expecting something more from his cousins, some explanation.

Josh kept glancing at Jason, the tip of his tongue flicking across his lips as if the two of them shared an exciting secret. He asked Michael, "You ever been tickled? I mean, *really* tickled?"

"No." Michael remembered one time when he saw two boys tickling an older boy in a secluded part of the local picnic grounds. The older boy was bigger and stronger but the smaller boys had caught him by surprise. In no time they had him spread out on the ground with all four of their hands up under his t-shirt. The older boy laughed and screamed and kicked, but it was no use. Michael had watched, unseen, feeling an excitement between his legs, until the tickled boy finally stopped struggling, his high-pitched laughter subsided to desperate panting, and a dark stain spread through the crotch of his jeans. At the time Michael didn't know what to make of the way that scene made him feel, but he never forgot it and often thought about it just before he went to sleep. The excitement between his legs, the way it felt against the sheets, the memory of those hands moving under the boy's shirt, hiking it up, exposing his hairy belly….

Michael looked at his cousins' hands, big and scarred and heavy, and could not picture them touching him. Were they really going to try?

Jason stepped forward. "Ain't nothing you can do about it," he said.

Josh stepped forward too, the cousins moving apart from each other, as if preparing to block Michael if he tried to run to either side. But he couldn't move, there was something unavoidable in the way they closed in on him, their faces perfectly serious, as if they had rehearsed this many times and were determined to spend all of their concentration on it.

Michael laughed nervously as his cousins reached out to him, and he drew his arms close to his body, instinctively protecting his ribs. "Look, I don't think I want to do this, okay?" He made his move toward the door.

"C'mon. We just wanna see if you're ticklish."

[33]

"I'm not, I'm not!" He was dismayed to hear how his voice squealed, as if they were already tickling him and it was true that he really, really couldn't stand it.

"Oh, c'mon…." By now both boys were running their fingers lightly up and down his arms. Michael couldn't stop giggling, partly from fear and partly because of these *feelings*…he didn't know that the light touch of fingers could be so unbearable, even through the sleeves of his plaid shirt. "Stop it!"

"Oh yeah, we'll have to tie you up all right," Josh said. "You're too ticklish."

"No! You can't!" Michael backed away, but soon he was up against a wall.

"In just a minute or two," Jason said, "you'll be *begging* us to tie you up." He and his brother began tickling Michael in earnest, prying against his arms where they so desperately tried to protect his ribs.

Michael was in a panic as he began to laugh and shout. The shock waves rushing through him took his breath away, and he had to explain, tell them that he was too ticklish, they had to stop. But he was laughing too much and he couldn't speak a word, though he kept trying to struggle. Now the attacking hands were going wild, touching, grabbing, poking him everywhere. Time slowed down somehow, seconds on the clock replaced by sensations that moved much faster, so that whenever he was able to catch his breath it seemed that hours had passed. But time, like Michael, wasn't going anywhere.

Once he managed to break away and scramble wide-eyed across the floor, but they caught him easily, and he realized he should have jumped out the window when he had the chance.

"Keep tickling him," Jason told his brother. "I'll be right back."

Josh straightened up from where he had been pinning

Michael's arms to the floor, and he fitted his hands to Michael's ribcage, creating sensations that made Michael limp with agony, unable to do anything but beg, when he could find breath, for his cousin to stop.

"You're squirming around too much," Josh said. "We'll fix that."

Jason returned to the room and closed the door behind him, and Josh stopped long enough for Michael to blink tears from his eyes and look up and see that Jason was holding a length of rope. "You're not…gonna tie me up," he panted.

"We have to," Jason said. "You move around too much."

"Yeah. This'll make it easier," Josh said. "You'll see."

Michael fought them, kicking, punching, even clawing them with his nails, but it was no use. Jason and Josh were nipping at his ticklish sides now. "We can do this the easy way, or the hard way," Josh said. "It doesn't matter which, because either way we'll get what we want."

With great effort Michael got a few words out: "N…no! Stop… please!"

"All right, then, we'll just keep tickling you till you let us tie you up."

Their hands massaged his ribs, prodded his belly, poked up into his armpits. He was growing too weak to try to push them away or even try to defend himself. But they *had* to understand that they couldn't keep tickling him! He managed to get to his feet again but it was useless, their hands followed him and he sank to the floor.

"The only way we'll stop," Josh said, "is if you'll let us tie you up."

Out of breath and desperate, Michael could only shake his head.

"Okay, then. You're asking for it." They unbuttoned Michael's shirt. He already felt so violated that he couldn't believe they were just now getting down to his bare skin. He tried again to struggle but they kept tickling, tickling him right out of his shirt. When their fingers attacked his bare armpits Michael shouted with laughter, his mouth stretched wide. The laughter was only encouraging them but he couldn't stop.

"Let us tie you up," Josh said. He was now tickling Michael's armpits while Jason tickled and teased Michael's sides just below his ribs.

Red in the face, gasping for breath, Michael shook his head.

"You're a glutton for punishment," Jason said. "That's okay, we've got all the time in the world." He put an iron grip on Michael's thighs, squeezing and squeezing as Michael screamed himself hoarse. The fingers moved farther up, closer to Michael's groin, and squeezed even harder. At the same time Josh was tickling deep in Michael's armpits, and the combination of tortures made him feel that he was falling, falling an impossibly long distance. If he didn't break the fall, he'd die.

"Please," he said finally, croaking out the words in desperation, "please, please."

His cousins both spoke at once. "Please, what?"

"Please tie me up."

"Do you mean it?" Jason's fingers moved up to either side of Michael's groin and squeezed.

Michael couldn't fathom the *unbearableness* of it. His tongue broke loose, it started babbling, he couldn't stop it. "Please tie me up, please please, do whatever you want, tie my hands, tie me up tight so I can't get away, *do it*, tie me up, whatever you want...."

Of course by then they could have tied him up anyway without encountering much of a struggle. But at least he got some relief

[36]

from the tickling while they tied his wrists together behind his back, then his ankles. They finished off by tying a third length of rope around his legs, just below his knees.

"Okay, guys," Michael said when they were through binding him, his voice weak and hoarse. "You've had your fun, now let me go."

Josh grinned. "You're not goin' anywhere, pal."

"Wh—what are you going to do?" They *couldn't* be planning on tickling him anymore, they *couldn't*! He knew well enough, though, that while they were tying his ankles together his sneakers and socks had come off. He was now naked to the waist *and* barefoot *and* unable to move.

"We still got a couple of hours before Ma gets home," Jason said. "Plenty of time to find *all* your ticklish spots."

Michael was so afraid he felt dizzy. "Don't touch me, please don't touch me! Look, I'll do anything you want, just let me go!"

"Anything we want?" Josh asked.

"Anything we want?" his brother chimed in. "Hey, that just might work!"

"Anything!" Michael said. "I mean it!"

"Well, what we want...."

"...is to *tickle you to death*!"

Michael screamed. They were on him, stroking and poking his belly as he twisted and turned, trying to escape their fingers. His laughter came fast and breathless, and along with the overwhelming sensations came the terror of seeing his cousins' faces, how they were grinning, enjoying themselves so much they might never stop.

By the time they had fully explored Michael's ticklish torso he was no longer sure where or who he was, and his laughter was little more than hysterical whispering controlled by his cousins' tireless hands gaining access to every inch of skin. They even took turns torturing his bellybutton with fingers they'd moistened in their mouths.

Just when he thought he might pass out, the tickling stopped. Oh, thank God! The guys had had their fun, he had somehow lived through it, and they would never do this to him again!

Blinking through tears, he realized that, though they had stopped tickling him, he was still pinned to the floor. Jason was sitting astride his waist, and Josh…well, Josh was nowhere to be seen. Maybe he had just gotten totally bored and went off to do something else.

It was a very slight sensation, no more than a mere pinprick against the sole of his foot, that gave Michael the first inkling of what was to come. He jumped, and Josh, out of sight but somewhere *down there*, gave a giggle.

In his delirium Michael had forgotten all about his feet. They had never been tickled, but if the tiny sensation that he'd just felt was any indication, he didn't *want* them to be, they *couldn't* be. He looked with dead seriousness into Jason's eyes and said, "Jason, don't let him tickle my feet. Please. I'll do whatever you guys want, swear to God."

Jason was shaking his head, his eyes glassy, a smile playing at his lips. "You still don't get it, do you?" He leaned over and began to rake his fingers down Michael's sides. "This *is* what we want. And we *will* do it. *All* the time."

Michael was laughing again, and his laughter grew shrill and piercing as Jason continued to tickle his sides and Josh continued to discover how wildly ticklish a pair of bare feet could be.

After a while Michael, who had all but lost his voice, was so weak and exhausted he didn't know if he'd ever be able to move again. But he didn't have to worry about that; after untying his

[38]

wrists and ankles his cousins moved him themselves, dragging him down the hall to the bedroom.

"No…," Michael croaked, "…what are you doing…?"

They threw him down on his bed and stripped off his jeans and underwear. Somewhere, in that part of him where he could still track what was happening, Michael felt mortified, for during the tickling his dick had gotten very hard and very wet. There was no way to hide it, he was horribly exposed as they tied him spread-eagle to his bed. When the last knot was cinched and he was feeling, for the first time, the panic of having his arms and legs stretched in this most vulnerable position, he twisted his head to see what his cousins were doing and faced an amazing sight: the two older boys were stripping off their shirts, exposing the muscular, hairy chests and abs that Michael had first seen the night before. Their jeans and underwear went next, and then they were standing naked on either side of the bed, their own hard-ons huge and dripping.

"So you got a woody too," Jason said. "Wonder if it'll get any bigger if we tickle you some more? Like for an hour, maybe, without stopping."

Not content with having pushed him to the edge of complete hysteria, the boys worked even harder now to drive him crazy with their fingers, grabbing and prying at his ribs and armpits, scratching at the soles of his feet.

Later, as they were teaching him how to jack them off exactly the way they liked it, and they were panting and twitching and saying that he hadn't felt *anything* yet, Michael wondered dimly how much more tickling he could take before they really did tickle him to death.

***

Michael's first Saturday with the cousins was sunny and warm, more like July than September. They took him to the middle of a huge field, taunting him all along the way: "We ain't even *started* tickling you yet." Michael was still dazed from the after-school sessions that had continued throughout the week. At night the tickle torture lasted long past bedtime, long past the point when he thought he would truly expire; Jason and Josh nearly broke his bed by crawling into it and squeezing him tight between their nakedness, their hands tickling him everywhere at once, their hard dicks pressing against him. They warned him that he'd better not make too much noise and wake Aunt Helen or he'd *really* get it. The press of their bodies, the ceaseless probing of their hands, the whispered threats, the tang of their sweat and the slapping of their wet dicks sent Michael into a delirium where he wasn't always sure if he was asleep or awake.

In the middle of the field, with no one else in sight as far as the eye could see, they stripped him naked and laid him down in the wild grass. There was no need, they explained, to tie his wrists and ankles out here, because even if he did manage to get to his feet and run there was nowhere to go—no rooms to hide in or doors to close, nothing to stop them from catching him and tickling him even more as punishment for trying to escape. Michael could only moan in fear as Josh kneeled down behind his head and held his arms while Jason straddled him just above the waist and went to work on his ribcage.

As Michael laughed and screamed he kept his eyes on the blue sky above him, where a few bright clouds seemed almost close enough to touch. A tiny part of his mind that was not yet consumed by ticklish agony fastened on those clouds as if they might be his means of escape, and he yelled to them as they made their slow way across the sun. One wedge-shaped cloud became, as he stared at it, the immense white hull of a ship that was coming to pick him up and take him away, into the blue sky and beyond, far beyond the reach of his cousins' hands.

They tickled him for hours, stopping only in the late afternoon when the sky grew overcast and threatened rain. They got him up off the ground and forced him, exhausted as he was, to get his clothes back on—some strategic tickling helped with that process—and made their way back to the farmhouse. Michael was giggling all the way, he didn't know if he would ever stop. He kept touching himself here and there—he couldn't help it—because he didn't believe his skin could be so tender. At least today they had let him relieve the terrible aching between his legs—had even marveled at the amount of cum he could shoot. But when they tickled him *after* that...oh, Jesus, it was worse than ever!

As they approached the house Jason whispered to him, "Play it cool, Ma's home."

Aunt Helen was home ... an idea formed in Michael's addled head, a simple plan that just might save his life. As soon as they got in the house he would run to his aunt and throw himself at her mercy. He would beg her to keep Jason and Josh away from him, or at least to get them to stop tickling him. He would tell her that he couldn't stand it anymore, and she would know that he was telling the truth.

The kitchen smelled of apples and cinnamon and soap. Aunt Helen was at the sink, washing dishes. Quickly, before his cousins could stop him, Michael summoned what little energy he had left, ran across the room and threw his arms around his aunt's waist. He was ashamed to go to her like this, his face red from crying, his voice hoarse from screaming, and his jeans sticking to the cum on his legs; but nothing could keep him from clinging to

[41]

her, pressing into her floury apron as he begged her: "Make them stop… don't let them … no more…."

Michael's aunt put her hands on his shoulders. She patted his back as his tears dampened her apron. Her touch was soothing, but when he looked up at her he saw no surprise on her face, or even concern. She only smiled as she always did—as if she had expected him to come to her like this.

"I see the boys have been having their fun," she said.

"*Fun* … no … they've been … *tickling* me! Make them stop…!"

His aunt shook her head, chuckling. "Why, Michael, what are you talking about? That's what we brought you here for! Your cousins have to have their fun, after all. And poor little Dred Junior, he just couldn't take any more."

"D … Dred Junior? What…?"

She shook her head, and now there was a touch of sadness in her smile. "Poor thing, there was hardly anything left of him when they came to take him away."

Suddenly Michael heard a sound he was very familiar with by now: his cousins standing by the kitchen door, giggling. Michael let his arms drop from his aunt's waist. As he looked into her eyes, he saw now that they weren't quite right, somehow not quite right at all.

"Don't worry, Michael," she said, turning back to her dishes. "You're a good, strong boy. You'll last a long time."

***

Sunday was Michael's one day of rest, but on Monday, after school, the tickling started again. In the second floor room that had been empty a week ago Jason and Josh had installed a square wooden frame that could stand upright or lie flat on the floor, as it did now. After stripping him naked they dragged him into the frame. By now Michael was so sensitized that he laughed hysterically even while they were tying him up, even though they weren't tickling him at the time—or so they pretended. "Whoops, sorry, Michael," Jason said as a loose end of rope swept across Michael's belly, raising the pitch of his laughter. "Yeah, sorry, kid," Josh said as the rope he was using to tie his ankle slipped over his foot and slid along his sole, while Michael sputtered and the back of his head bounced against the floor. By the time they were finished tying him up his arms were above his head, wrists stretched toward two corners of the frame, and his ankles were raised up—fastened with ropes tied to those upper corners of the frame also—up and nearly over Michael's head. This humiliating position made him newly vulnerable, his ass raised up off the floor and his asshole exposed, and he thought, *here it comes, they're gonna rape me*, but they had a different kind of violation in mind, with different tools: some short, stiff feathers that they passed briefly across Michael's field of vision before they started brushing lightly against the backs of Michael's thighs and his asscheeks, and he was learning still more about tickle torture than he'd ever dreamed he'd know. All that sensitive skin around his asshole, between his legs, beneath his balls, all of it never touched before, not like this .... Michael moaned and laughed and babbled, begging his cousins to fuck him if that's what they really wanted to do, knowing all the while they'd do what they wanted whether he told them to or not.

"Who's our pussy?" they kept asking. "Who's our pussy?"

"I'm your pussy!" Michael hollered. "I'm your pussy! I am!" His position, accompanied by his own dripping hard-on riding high on his belly, raised his feelings of helplessness to a new level.

When a car pulled into the dooryard, tires crunching

ferociously on gravel, it meant that their mother was home and they would soon have to be ready for dinner. But after a sneak peek through the window the boys went back to tormenting their cousin as if nothing had happened. To Michael's surprise the front door soon *slammed* so hard that it couldn't be Aunt Helen who had just come in.

"The traveling man's home! Where's my family?" The booming voice of Uncle Dred, who had been on the road for weeks, was followed by the *whump* of his suitcases hitting the floor. When heavy footsteps sounded on the stairs Michael thought his cousins would surely stop, but they didn't—not even when the door banged open and Uncle Dred stood in the doorway with his hands on his hips. He was a big man with a deep chest, broad shoulders and dark hair covering his brawny arms.

"Hey, Pop," Jason said, his evil grin widening as he probed Michael's armpits.

To the extent that he could concentrate on anything, Michael tried to picture what this scene must look like to his uncle. To find his two teenage sons buck naked, tormenting their cousin, who was also naked, all three boys with raging hard-ons ... surely Uncle Dred would be raring to get out the razor strop and beat them to within an inch of their lives. *Help*, Michael tried to say, but he was laughing too hard. *Help me...!* After several tries he managed to get a few words out: "Help ... they're tickling me to death!"

Uncle Dred's posture was stern as he stood there with his hands on his hips. But his face ... was he *grinning*? "Well, well, well," he said at last. "You've done a good job here, boys. You've got your cousin fixed up real good."

"Help, help!" Michael rasped. "I can't take it...."

"I can see that, son," Uncle Dred said. His tongue licked the corner of his mouth. When he finally raised his hand it wasn't to strike anyone, but to fumble with the buttons of his white shirt. The hair on his chest, dense and swirling like the hair on his arms, burst forth as the buttons gave way. He pulled the unbuttoned shirt free of his pants and shucked it off, then unbuckled his belt. As soon as his pants slid down his muscular thighs he grabbed the band of his badly distended briefs and pulled them down too. His enormous cock pointed straight at Michael, just like his eyes as he said, "Bring his legs down, boys. Let's get him spread-eagle. Michael, I can tell by the look on your face that you're ticklish just about everywhere, am I right?"

Uncle Dred didn't need to be told, he soon found out for himself. His big hands, all on their own, could do as much as his sons' four hands had done; and when all six hands were working him over they took Michael to a new place, farther out on the thin edge of reality, closer to the great darkness beyond.

It was then that Michael heard the voices for the first time. They were like a choir, male and female voices perfectly understandable and yet, he knew, unheard by the others. *Someday, Michael*, they sang. *Someday you will have the power.* He thought he saw where the voices were coming from—a cloud shaped like the prow of a ship, cleaving a pure blue sky.

***

While Jason and Josh spent most of their spare time tormenting Michael's ticklish skin in every way they could think of, at school they played a different role, as Michael's protectors. There were plenty of bullies around, but Jason and Josh saw to it that no one else ever laid hands on him. Any boys who accidentally discovered Michael's weakness pursued it no further, knowing they would have to answer to his cousins.

One afternoon, when Michael had stayed after class to get help from his algebra teacher, he was crossing the nearly empty parking lot when someone whistled to him. He tried to make out who was standing in the shadows over by the gym entrance. He began walking in that direction, then stopped when he saw who it was: Bill Logan, a big, brawny senior with a reputation for picking on freshmen. Michael shared a gym class with Logan, but even there he did his best to keep away from the older boy.

"Hey, you," Logan called to him now. "C'mon over here."

Logan's voice was so typically loud that Michael couldn't pretend not to hear him, any more than he could pretend to think that Logan was calling to someone else, since there was no one else around. Paralyzed by dread, Michael could only stand there till Logan called again.

"Hey, you!"

Logan didn't even know his name. Without moving any closer Michael called, "What do you want?"

"Come over here."

"I can't. I'm late."

"You'll get over here if you know what's good for you."

Once again Michael surveyed the empty parking lot. Where were his cousins when he really needed them? Having no choice, he began walking toward Logan.

Logan stood on the stairs that led down to the gym's side entrance, which was one floor below ground level. So from Michael's vantage point he was only visible from the waist up. Still his broad chest and shoulders gave him all the authority he needed as he yelled "Speed it up!"

Michael double-timed it to the top of the stairs, where he stood breathless, more from fear than from running. When his eyes adjusted to the shade and he got a full view of Logan he stopped breathing completely.

Logan was leaning against the wall with his fly open and his very considerable dick in his hand.

"Get down here, you fruit," he said. "I got something for you to suck on."

Michael took a step back. *Fruit?* He had never been called that before. *Fag* or *faggot*, maybe, but only in the joking way that boys his age used those words. Logan's insult cut deep, accompanied as it was by the visual aid that was growing longer and thicker in his hand; Michael had glimpsed it many times in the locker room after gym class, but never in this excited state.

"I said *get down here*. You're going to suck me off, and like it."

Michael couldn't move—not forward, because he was so scared of Logan, and not backward, because he was so fascinated by that dick that stood out like a stanchion between Logan's legs. All he could think was, *I'm doomed. I'm doomed.*

It was then that Jason and Josh came running around the corner of the gym building, as if Michael's stress had sounded an alarm. They rushed past Michael on either side and down the steps, all the way to the bottom, dragging Logan with them. Big as he was, Logan was too startled to resist. On the concrete landing by the gym's darkened door, Josh stood behind Logan, his arm around the bully's neck, while Jason pulled out his pocketknife and unsheathed its four-inch blade. He grabbed Logan's dick and poised the blade at the root of its thick shaft. "You're about to lose your best asset, you prick!"

Logan's eyes grew wide with terror. "*No!* Oh Jesus Christ, *don't!*"

Michael stared at the tableau at the bottom of the steps, where all three boys seemed frozen in time. Nothing moved except

Logan's chest as he panted in terror.

Finally Jason said, "You're never gonna bother Michael again."

"I … I wasn't bothering nobody! This was all his idea! He said he wanted to … to suck me off!"

Jason glanced up the stairs. "Is that true?"

"No!" Michael said. "He was going to make me do it."

Jason turned back to Logan. "True?" he asked, and the blade must have moved ever so slightly, for Logan's eyes grew even wider and he yelled, "Okay! Okay! It's true! I was gonna make him! Don't, oh Jesus *don't*...."

"You know what else?" Michael asked, his voice rising. "He called me a fruit."

"He *what?*" That was Josh speaking, tightening his hold on Logan's throat.

"That does it," Jason said, and Logan squealed in terror. But Jason stepped back, folded the knife, and put it back in his pocket. "I won't cut you, Logan," he said, "but we *will* give you something to remember us by."

Now that the knife was gone Logan struggled anew. "Let me go...."

"Not till we find out something," Jason said.

In a move that combined dexterity with strength, Josh released his armhold around Logan's neck and then, in a flash, grabbed his arms instead, holding them behind Logan's back.

Very casually Jason placed his fingers at the bully's sides. "You ticklish, Logan? Huh?"

Logan's eyes grew wide again, just for a second. "Let me go, you faggot!"

"Oh, that was a mistake!" Jason let his fingers play lightly up and down Logan's sides.

Logan did his best not to laugh. Instead he held his breath, and his face grew more and more red as Jason intensified the tickling at either side of Logan's belly, then up onto his ribs.

Logan began to sputter, his face redder than ever. Finally he managed to say, "Stop! Stop it!"

"Stop what?" Jason asked. "I'm not doing anything to you." But even as he spoke he was pushing up Logan's sweatshirt, exposing his hairy belly and ribs. "That's better. I like to see where I'm going." He began to explore those ribs more thoroughly, prodding and squeezing each one, then tickling rapidly up and down as he continued to taunt Logan. "How's this, buddy? Ever been tickled so much you can't even fight anymore? That's when it *really* gets bad, Logan. That's when you *really* can't stand it. You'd do *anything* to stop it, but you can't."

By now Logan was laughing, a rapid breathless giggling interspersed with begging: "Don't ... don't do this to me ... *please* don't ... I'm begging you...."

Jason's fingers went wild now, tickling all over Logan's torso and belly, probing his abs, poking his navel. "I like that, Logan, I like to hear you beg. You'll be begging a lot more before we're through with you."

"Let me tickle him now," Josh said. "Let me, let me."

"Wait just a minute, brother. I'm going to tickle him helpless, then we can both do what we want ... isn't that right, Logan? When you're too weak to fight back we can *really* get at you. Both of us at once. We'll tickle the shit out of you."

Logan struggled harder than before, almost breaking Josh's grip. But that brief effort cost him all his strength. His knees weakened and he began to sag in Josh's arms. This gave Jason a chance to push his sweatshirt up even higher, so he could reach under it and get Logan's armpits. This had a galvanic effect on Logan. His laughter became high pitched, almost a squeal.

[49]

"That gets you where you live, doesn't it, Logan? I think I'll tickle your armpits for an *hour*, how would you like that?"

As the bully sank to his knees, Josh released his grip on Logan's arms and grabbed his sweatshirt instead, pulling it completely off. Then he and Jason both worked on Logan's torso as he squealed and screamed and begged, his legs thrashing erratically, his semi-hard dick flopping wildly against his jeans.

At the top of the steps, Michael watched in fascination. He longed to join in, to get his own hands on Logan's ticklish flesh, and his longing grew as his cousins exposed more and more of Logan's big frame. But he didn't dare leave his vantage point, where he could keep one eye on the parking lot to make sure it stayed empty. It was incredible how fast and how far his cousins' hands could work; in what seemed like seconds they had not only spread Logan out flat on the concrete but had also removed his sneakers, socks, jeans, and underwear. Now that their tickling victim was buck naked the two boys could explore him thoroughly. Josh straddled Logan, his knees pinning the older boy's forearms to the ground, and practiced his rapid tickling technique on those fatally sensitive armpits as Logan clawed at the concrete till his nails were ground down and his fingertips bled. Meanwhile Jason worked on Logan's sides and belly, inducing more and more intense states of panic in his victim, whose wildly rolling eyes seemed to be searching for answers: What if Jason kept working downward, toward his groin, where he had never been tickled before? What if those strong, relentless fingers reached those tender spots where his groin met his thighs...? He didn't have to wait long to find out. His laughter reached an insane pitch as Jason's fingers violated his groin, not neglecting his heavy, ticklish balls.

Michael, meanwhile, was also wondering: how long would it

take to tickle Logan completely helpless? The cousins had been working him over for what seemed like a long time already, and from the way Logan's body twitched and heaved it looked as if he still had some fight left in him. Michael got his answer, though, as Jason hunkered down between Logan's legs and worked on those inner thighs while Josh kept at his armpits. At first Logan bucked more furiously than ever, but after a few minutes he began to sag, his legs ceasing their struggle. Michael noted with satisfaction that the bully's full-throated laughter was now completely gone, replaced by a breathless stream of giggling as he grew weaker by the second.

"We're breaking him!" Josh cried, and Jason, who was sweating with effort, said, "Don't stop now!"

This was quite a sight—Bill Logan naked and helpless, his cock that was fully hard again swinging through the air like a speedometer needle out of control. Having immobilized his victim to the point where he could hardly move, Jason crept slowly down, down from Logan's thighs to his knees, then his calves, then on down toward his feet....

In desperation Logan rallied one last time, raising his head and squealing, just like a girl: "No! No! Don't tickle my feet!"

"Just what I wanted to hear," Jason said. He lay down on the concrete and put an armlock on Logan's ankles. The soles of those big tender feet flexed and squirmed, but they were no match for Jason's skilled fingers. Logan kept squealing as Jason made those soles his complete property, from the heels to the toes to the spaces between those toes. It didn't help that Josh had finally left those tortured armpits and had moved on to the boy's upper ribs.

Michael continued to keep one fearful eye on the parking lot and one fascinated eye on the action below him. Though his cousins had reduced him to a helpless, blubbering state on many occasions, he had never seen it done to someone else—the memory he had of the tickled boy at the picnic grounds was nothing compared to this. Watching his cousins work, he had to admire their strength and agility, moving over Logan like accomplished gymnasts. They could do anything they wanted, handling the boy like a big piece of meat, rolling him over to explore his back. Logan panted heavily, his voice, whenever he managed to find it, reduced to delirious croaks and whispers. Michael didn't want to desert his post but had to move a few steps downward so he could make out some of the words:

"Don't ... don't do this anymore ... I'm gonna die ... I'll do anything, I swear to God ... I'll suck your dicks ... all three of you ... and I won't tell nobody, ever, I swear!"

Those last words caught Jason's attention. "What's that supposed to mean, you won't tell nobody? Does that mean it ever entered your head that you *might* tell? You'll pay for that!" And Jason found, much to his delight, that Logan's lower back was almost as ticklish as his feet. Exhausted as he was, Logan stiffened and squealed again and again as if Jason's fingers were sparking off electric shocks.

"Here, try this," Jason said to his brother, who eagerly moved down from Logan's shoulder blades to the tender tapered area at the base of the boy's spine while Jason alternately grabbed his firm butt checks and squeezed the hell out of the backs of his thighs. Logan's was struggling so to cry out that he was nearly gagging: "Please! Please! I'll do anything...!"

Jason moved up to the boy's head, cupped Logan's chin in his hand and turned it to look him in the eye. "You'll do anything, huh? Is that right?" As if to refresh Logan's memory Jason let his free hand roam along Logan's ribs, up into his right armpit.

"Oh, Jesus God, yes! Anything!"

burst through their jeans. There was no one in sight as far as they could see, and they weren't likely to meet anyone; finally Michael couldn't stand it anymore, he unzipped his fly and pulled his hard dick free, letting it sway before him. Then he grabbed Jason's crotch, pulled his wet heavy dick into the light. Then Josh's. Without saying anything the three of them made their way, cock-heavy, panting slightly, over the empty fields toward home, under what was left of the afternoon sun.

***

Jason and Josh—and Uncle Dred, when he was home—spent most of their spare time tickling Michael over the next two years, while the house fell more and more into disrepair, weeds took over the garden and the dooryard, and Aunt Helen continued her chores in the kitchen, humming to herself as she took fresh pies from the oven.

Somehow Michael lasted. His aunt was right, he was a strong boy and seemed able to survive any amount of tickling punishment. It helped that the voices came back, often when he needed them most, with their reassurances: *Don't panic, Michael. Don't give up. Someday you'll have the power.*

But nothing stayed the same for very long, and after a while Jason and Josh began to seek out fresh victims at the high school. They had never forgotten their afternoon with Bill Logan and were curious about other boys who, in turn, were curious about what the good-looking brothers might want from them. By the time the victims found out, to their agonized dismay, they had been robbed of their clothes, their dignity, and a good part of their sanity.

Jason was working full-time as a mechanic, and was able to buy a second-hand car. The brothers expanded their territory, roaming the countryside looking for young men to tickle, venturing as far as the rest stop on the interstate, where they hit pay dirt. There were plenty of guys who were easy to lure into Jason's back seat ... guys who wouldn't object to a short trip through the countryside, not if it got them next to these big handsome boys ... guys who wouldn't hesitate to enter the abandoned shack in the woods that Jason and Josh had found and rigged up for their games. By the time their victims saw the stout oak table fitted with shackles, it was too late.

Michael found that he enjoyed working out with weights. Strenuous curls and presses seemed to relieve some of the anger he carried, that would sometimes break out in blind rages during which his cousins had learned to leave him alone. But most of the time when the rages came on Michael was by himself; and he had to admit that the anger had something to do with the fact that his cousins *weren't* tormenting him the way they used to. Even when they took him out to the shack and tortured him for an entire weekend, Michael was aware that there had been other guys in that shack, many of them; and now it wasn't the same with his cousins, not like it used to be.

When he was old enough, Michael ran away and joined the Navy. He had never forgotten that afternoon when his cousins had stripped him naked in the field and he had seen the white hull of a ship in the clouds, a ship that would take him away. He longed for a new world—one that would teach him many new things, and draw him nearer to the power his voices had promised him.

In the Navy Michael found he didn't have much in common with the scarcely grown boys that surrounded him, but he soon learned ways of meeting other guys who had extreme tastes for unusual practices. Many of them were into bondage, and knew more than Michael had ever thought possible to know about materials and tools, knots and positions. It was a science, a fully developed discipline. Some of these guys were also into tickling, and wouldn't hesitate to demonstrate techniques they'd picked up in various parts of the world. Laughing, begging and screaming, Michael often had the intuition that his cousins, who had once seemed all-powerful and all-knowing, were just amateurs after all. Still, he found himself missing them, missing that part of the country where his erotic life had begun. After two tours of duty he headed back again. His cousins had also left the farm by that time, and his uncle and aunt would soon be moving into a retirement home. Michael found work and held onto the farm. He had a lot to do.

3. THE COMPOUND

I came to on the floorboard of Michael's truck, inside a sack of some kind, its coarse weave brushing against my skin, making me twitch and gasp as we sped over rough roads. Confined as I was, I couldn't believe that he still wasn't coming at me with his fingers and tongue and tools. In this newfound darkness I could smell only my own moist body, hear only the straining engine and gravel spitting against the fenders; but very slowly I began to see, and what I saw were pictures from Michael's life story. I saw his cousins, two oversexed boys with too much time on their hands; I saw his uncle, a strapping wildman who had Michael in the palm of his hand; I even saw his Aunt Helen, stooping to take a pie from the oven as Michael's screams of laughter came through the kitchen ceiling. I saw the country, the junk cars and rotting silos, the huge high school where kids from four counties were herded together like cattle. I saw Bill Logan, whose life was changed forever on the afternoon he spent in the cousins' custody. I saw the cloud that took on the shape of a boat, and heard the heavenly choir that told Michael what to do.

Michael had told me his story—or variations of his story, some filled with much more detail than others—while he was tickling me. He kept me tied hand and foot for a good while, lying there on the floor of a bare room in the farmhouse he had dragged me to; I wondered why he had no equipment, no stocks or torture racks or even a platform where a slave could be tied spread-eagle. Then I realized that this was how he himself had been introduced to extreme tickle torture, in a room bare of furnishings. This may even have been the room that his cousins first took him to so long ago.

When he finally freed my ankles it was because he had tickled my lower ribs for so long that I'd lost control of my bladder and pissed my pants. After untying the ropes he undid my jeans and stripped them off. There was no danger that I would try to run; by then I was so weak I couldn't even stand up. He half-carried, half-dragged me into a bathroom and stood me under the shower for a few minutes. Then, since we were taking a break anyway and he didn't want me to die—not of starvation, anyway—he gave me some cold cereal and some water.

He took me to a different room. At first I was glad because my muscles were sore from struggling and thrashing on the hardwood floor. But this new room did have equipment, including a pair of stocks where my feet could be bound with my toes pointing downward, then the toes spread and bound one by one so ingeniously that they had never been so exposed. I wondered how long I could stand to have my feet tickled in that position, but it was idle wondering, because whatever would happen to me next had no relation to the length of time I could stand it.

As it turned out Michael spent several hours on my feet. I was as good as blindfolded, since I was lying on my belly and could not turn my head enough to see him—what he was doing, what he was about to do, what instrument he would use next. My world consisted entirely of the ticklishness of my feet; the rest of what existed, like the rest of me—screaming, bawling, thrashing—was totally useless.

Michael seemed very pleased when he finally unbound my feet. He had reduced me to a drooling idiot, trembling and twitching, panting, and whimpering, unable to keep my tongue inside my mouth. When he looked at me with those narrow-set blue eyes, I could see what he was seeing—a broken wreck who was now good for only one thing, to be tickled and tickled until the tormentor himself was nearly dead from exhaustion.

"Oh, my friend…I'll go back to your ribs next," Michael said. "That should be good for another half day, at least."

Michael's most ingenious device was a rack with restraints attached to a fiendishly responsive system of ropes and pulleys. It was rigged to punish a victim for struggling; if I tried, for example, to flex my feet against a deadly attack on my soles, the rack would "sense" my struggle and a weight would drop to tighten the cords that kept my toes tied back, so that my soles would be even more immovable, more exposed than before. If I tried to pull my arms down in an attempt to guard my ribs or armpits, the leather grips around my wrists would move upward, stretching my arms even farther, till my ribs nearly burst through my skin and my armpits felt like they were turned inside out. I soon understood my limited options: I could be torn limb from limb, or tickled to death, or both.

I had to learn to stay completely still as the madman did whatever he wanted to me, each change in strategy prefaced by those words: *Oh, my friend….*

***

I wasn't sure how I had got in the sack on the floor of Michael's truck, or for how long I'd been there. I only knew I was going somewhere. I tried to speak his name, but could summon up no more than a whisper. Then I fell into a deep sleep, for in spite of my cramped position my body cried out for rest, and for the first time in many hours—days?—I wasn't being tickled.

[59]

Sometime later the truck ground to a halt, waking me. "End of the line," Michael said, and in a moment the passenger's side door opened and I was moving, the sack being dragged through the door and then upended to dump me unceremoniously onto the ground. The bright early sun assaulted my eyes: maybe this was what it was like to be born, naked and squinting, not knowing where you were or what would come next.

I wasn't quite naked, since Michael had put my jeans on me, at least; but I felt totally naked as I lay on soft grass with about a dozen men and women looking down at me. Dressed mostly in denim, they seemed like country types. My urban upbringing had left me with a conviction that such people tended to be unwashed, inbred, and malevolent. I looked up into their curious faces, some of them smiling, most fairly young. Malevolent? Did that have to be true? Squinting, I could see that they could just as easily be missionaries, kind strangers who might reclaim me for the living now that I had been nearly tickled to death.

"Welcome to the Compound," Michael said in my direction, then turned to the others. "He's broken in real good. You won't have to keep him tied up all the time, he's too weak to go anywhere. Also I think his brains are a little scrambled by now."

I wanted to explain to them that my brains weren't scrambled, that I was perfectly aware of what was happening to me. I wanted to say something like, Good people, thank you for rescuing me from this madman. Take me in, show me my bed, and put this sadist in chains. But when I opened my mouth only a weak giggle came out.

One young man stretched out a bare foot to touch me. His toe lightly grazed my ribcage, and I heard myself shriek as I curled up into a ball like a caterpillar touched with a stick.

"You've got him broken in, all right!" someone hollered, and the laughter that followed revealed, in the way it rippled and spread across some unseen distance, that what I had first thought of as about a dozen people was actually a crowd.

A woman's voice piped up, firm and practical. "We'll let the children play with him first," she said.

Strong hands moved me to another patch of lawn. I was left alone lying on my back on the grass. The sun felt good, its touch kind and warm. See, I told myself, nothing bad is going to happen here.

In the distance a bell sounded, like a school bell, and it was almost as if I were a kid again, smelling the grass, feeling the sun, listening to sounds of feet on a paved path, happy kids eager to play. Only my body kept me rooted in the present, because the grass I was lying on, soft and yielding as it was, tickled my heels and ankles and legs and all the way up my spine to the back of my neck and behind my ears— so much so that I was laughing softly, continuously. As ticklish as I had been all my life, I had never been *this* ticklish.

The sounds of running feet and eager voices weren't just memories; there really were children approaching. Before I knew it they had surrounded me, their faces indistinct with the strong sun behind them as they stood giggling and jostling each other. Just these small children, no adults that I could see. But wait. If this was recess, shouldn't there be a playground monitor? Someone to supervise the play, to make sure all was fair, to prevent any childhood cruelties like bullying or shoving...or *tickling?*

There were a few things I thought I knew about kids. Number one, each child was intensely aware of his or her own ticklishness, which was bound to be exploited by another kid or some adult at one time or another. Number two, because of their size and their relative inability to defend themselves, most children knew what it was like to be *helpless* and tickled—the frustration and rage, the *unfairness* of it. This led to point number three: children respected the power of tickling and were less likely to wield it in a genuinely sadistic way. Even as I had these thoughts, however, I remembered an incident in my neighborhood when I was around thirteen, something that happened in the home of Old Man Abernathy, a grandfather figure to the little kids that played endlessly in the street. He always kept his screen door unlatched, and they were used to barging in and demanding jellybeans from the bag he kept next to his recliner.

On one particular summer morning I heard a commotion from Old Man Abernathy's house, and went up onto his porch and opened the screen door, something I had not done since I was a little kid myself. What I saw surprised me enough that I stood there in the open doorway for several minutes. About a dozen little kids, the oldest no more than seven or eight, surrounded the old man in his recliner, and they were all tickling him. He was in a helpless position, his chair tilted all the way back, and he was wearing only pajama trousers. Greedy little fingers ran up and down the old man's bare feet as more fingers got at his belly and ribs and armpits, all the places they knew damn well were most likely to be ticklish. The old man's mouth stretched wide in howling laughter, the exposed gray hair of his chest and underarms glowed in the sunlight through his picture window. His long bare feet were propped up nearly level with his head and held fast by several pairs of hands while busy fingers attacked them all over, not just the soles but also the toes and the tops of his feet. The kids were having the time of their lives, poking and squeezing and rubbing him everywhere, even his neck and behind his ears, as his laughter rose to an insane pitch, his eyes rolling wildly, tears running down his cheeks; when he managed to raise his head enough to see me, he tried to speak, though it took him several tries. Finally he gasped out, "Randy! Help me!"

I don't know how long I stood in that doorway before he begged for help, or how long I stood there after that, rooted to the spot. I'd never seen an adult tickled by kids like that, and it amazed me how shamelessly cruel they could be, using their fingernails on his belly and the soles of his feet, scratching at his ribs like wild rodents. I only know that at one point I finally closed the screen door behind me and crossed to the kitchen area, which was separated from the living room by a low counter. I was able to kneel down on the linoleum behind the counter and still see into the living room while I unzipped my jeans and pulled out my aching boner. It was the jackoff of my young life, kneeling there watching the old man get tickle-tortured to the point where his wild laughter subsided to a hysterical giggling, then grew silent as he panted and gasped, his tortured ribcage expanding like a bellows as he tried to draw in air. Meanwhile I worked my flying fist, beating off into my left hand till I shot so hard it stung my palm.

They tickled him till he passed out and they couldn't coax any more sensations from his abused skin. I was the last to leave the place, after making sure the old man was still breathing, and even before I made it to the front door and down the steps my dick was raising its head and I knew I'd have to jack off again soon, reliving the past half-hour or so with as much detail as I could summon.

Recalling that incident as I lay on the grass at the Compound, I saw in it something I had never seen before, not this clearly: the bone-chilling horror of being attacked by children who didn't know when to stop and didn't care. Sure, they were curious, I understood that; here's a half-undressed guy with bare feet sprawled on the grass, someone they'd never seen before. They would want to know where I came from and what I was doing there. I began to speak to them, trying to keep my hoarse, shaky voice gentle. "Listen, kids, there's only one thing I want you to remember, okay? I'm really ticklish, so don't touch me. Okay?" I tried to wet my lips, wishing I had a glass of water. "I've been treated very badly by a very bad man, he touched me where he shouldn't have for a very long time, he made me laugh and scream and it was really not nice, the way he treated me. But you kids, I know you're good kids, you've had a good upbringing and you wouldn't take advantage of a stranger who's…ticklish…."

They looked at me, nudging each other, smiling: boys and girls, all of grade school age, some of them barely older than toddlers. Surely I was right: with so many children there must be a responsible adult nearby, a teacher following the crowd, probably more than one teacher.

But suppose this *wasn't* a kind place. Suppose "we'll let the children play with him" meant something other than shooting marbles, drawing with chalk on the sidewalk, or choosing up sides for a ball game? The way they were giggling and jostling each other fed my paranoia. They seemed to know what was going to happen next, and I didn't.

"Kids?" If only I could get a sign from them, a friendly word. Then I realized I wasn't sure if I'd spoken aloud or not. Wouldn't it be terrifying if I hadn't connected at all, was nothing more than a juicy speechless stranger lying here, a grimy match to their grimy hands, as ready for consumption as a ripe banana? "Kids…?"

There must have been some signal that set them at me, though I didn't hear it. Soon there was nothing to hear but my own hysterical croaking, mixed with their excited laughter, childish greed driving them on to grab whatever part of me they could and tickle it for all they were worth. Of course it was *fun* for them, and that was the whole point, wasn't it? Except I had no sense that it was *only* fun, not the way they were going at me. There was nothing improvised here, nothing random in their aggression; this was part of their *lesson plan*. Since some of the younger ones were tickling a helpless man for the first time, the older boys and girls were even helping them, guiding their tiny fingers toward my most sensitive spots, showing them how to find my ribs, teaching them tickling games to play with my navel.

The little girls seemed to love my armpits the most. Michael had kept them shaved and slick and sensitized to the nth degree, and the girls found they could burrow into them with their delicate fingers, while I could do nothing because my arms were stretched tightly above my head and pinned down by many small hands. I howled and howled and, when I could find the breath for it, begged them to stop.

Meanwhile the boys, particularly the older ones, seemed most interested in my feet. With so many hands helping, it was easy to stretch my soles and spread my toes. With a kind of sadism that seems to come naturally to boys, they tickled my feet with as many things as they could find: the rough edges of coins and the teeth of pocket combs, crumpled foil wrappers from sticks of gum, bits of string that they quickly learned to pull between my toes. They used blades of grass, dandelion stems, and twigs and leaves they found lying around; and as soon as they found a spot that seemed particularly ticklish, they would run through their whole repertoire on that one tiny place, fingers and coins and combs and all, before searching for the next spot—like little scientists exhausting every possibility from one experiment before moving on to the next.

While several girls explored my armpits and a gang of boys

tortured my feet, the rest of my body was a free-for-all. Some of the kids invented a game where they held the littlest children over me, their bare feet dangling low enough for them to tickle my belly with their toes. Others were prying at my ribs as if they could force them apart and get deeper inside me, into my very *heart*. Sure, they would tickle that too if they could!

I was theirs for a long time.

***

At some point I was moved again. I was hardly in my right mind, but this time I noticed that the men carrying me were dressed alike, in gray coveralls and black boots. They took me into a room, stripped off my jeans, and stood me underneath a warm shower. It was my first chance to get clean in—how long? I couldn't say, couldn't work backward in time very far. There had been the children, of course, and before that the ride in the truck, and before that....

Without warning I was dragged from under the shower, wrapped in a towel, and tickled till I was dry and gasping for breath. Then I was shoved naked into a chair and fed some pieces of meat and bread. I had barely choked it down and followed it with a few sips of tepid water when the men in gray coveralls took me outside again. In an open area that looked like a village square, some stocks had been set up, and a bench with a wooden frame overhead. A crowd of women waited there; they wore denim work clothes, and had severe, unadorned looks. The men handed me over to them like a loaf of bread.

I had never been handled by women before, and the strength and efficiency of their movements amazed me. They sat me on the bench, fastened my ankles into the stocks, and tied my wrists over my head to the wooden frame. There was no awkwardness in their movements, as if they were used to stretching and arranging the limbs of naked male strangers. I asked them why they were doing this to me, and didn't get a glance in return. So I began to explain, in a trembling voice, that they were going to have to release me. I couldn't take any more of the kind of treatment I'd already received that day, if I were tickled any more I would die. In response to this, two of the women started tickling my belly.

"I like his belly," one said.

"Try over here," the other woman said. "No, here." Referring to a spot near my waist that made me shout. Her friend found the exact same spot on my other side. Neither of these women looked at my face or paid any attention as I begged them to stop. They were sensitive to my begging, though, because the more I begged the more they tickled the spots that were causing me to cry out. I squirmed as much as I could, which wasn't much. My dick moved, though—thickening, hardening, creeping up my belly as the women's fingers moved down, tickling along the length of my hard-on to my scrotum, where they applied their light, maddening touch to my balls. I broke into a harsh, steady laughter that called other adults, male and female, to gather around. They stared at the slender female fingers teasing and tormenting my balls. More hands appeared to tickle my inner thighs. Before long I was being poked and prodded just about everywhere.

I had plenty of time to learn how women ticklers differed from their male counterparts. In spite of the fact that so many of these women seemed to be work-toughened and strong, there was something different about their touch, which seemed to *linger* over my skin, each tickling stroke ending in a slight caress that was gentle and, at the same time, excruciating. It was as if the maternal impulse to smooth and soften were turned toward a different end. I had heard about men being tickled helpless by women, but I never knew what it was like until I felt my armpits, ribs, belly, and balls being fondled, then tickle-tortured, by female hands.

Meanwhile the men clustered around my feet like sharks at feeding time. My soles had been stretched, my toes expertly bound to the stocks so that no ticklish spot would be left unexplored, and before long there were more greedy hands on my feet than I had ever felt before. I raised my head and howled like a starving wolf at the edge of a frozen prairie, howled until there was nothing left of my voice but a high-pitched keening.

I was barely conscious when they finally freed my wrists and released my ankles from the stocks. Were they letting me go at last? Even in my delirium I wouldn't believe it. My flesh had ceased to exist except as their greedy hands defined it; if they loosened my bonds it was only because I was now so helpless that there was no point in restraining me. The hands never left me, not for a moment. They moved along my limbs, pried under my back, and turned me over, rearranging me so that they could tickle where they could not reach before, from the back of my neck down to my asshole.

**

Late that afternoon, after I'd had water and a few minutes' rest, the men in gray coveralls appeared again. They took me, still naked, into a large room and tied me to a table.

Soon the room began to fill with teenage boys. I would have expected, given the surroundings, that these would be mostly country boys—boys whose mothers cut their hair in their kitchens, who never drove anything but tractors and old pickups with hay clinging to the bumpers, who wouldn't know how to negotiate a crosswalk in a big city. But though there were some boys like that, there seemed to be other kinds too. All kinds. They milled naked around the large, semilit room of which I was the centerpiece, bound naked to a table. Nudity was more becoming to seventeen-year-old bodies than any garment—especially these bodies, so many of them tanned and chiseled, with dicks that stood unabashedly erect, straining toward the ceiling. Adrift in homoerotic savviness, they checked each other out with frank appraisal, and there was an earnestness in their murmuring, a *need* accompanied and driven by hip-hop from a boombox in the corner.

I was too keyed up, too frightened, too intimidated by the mix of voices and music to focus on anything but random details—a hand or face flashing by, a tongue flicking across lips. A pierced nipple, an illegible tattoo. And I realized, after listening to the voices for some time, why the mix was so confusing.

They were speaking in different languages.

Could it be? Or had I really lost my mind? No, that was unmistakable, nasal French coming from behind me, and some quick, clipped Spanish passing by. A couple of surprisingly deep voices seemed to be shouting across the room at each other in German. Forcing my eyes, which wanted to dart from corner to corner of the room like a trapped cat, to stay still for a moment to watch those passing by me, I could more easily see as well as hear the differences among them. The skin colors: whites, blacks, and browns. Asian boys casually stroking each other's nipples. Some Scandinavian boys looking at cards—with dirty pictures?—and chattering excitedly. Italian boys, each of them fondling his dick with one hand and talking with the other.

I was more frightened than ever. If it was true, if these were teenaged boys from all over the world, then that meant that this place was larger, more organized, more inescapable than I'd hoped.

I wondered how long they were going to ignore me, no more than casually glancing at the table as they passed by, grouping and regrouping. Was it possible that I was only there for them to *look* at, when and if they became interested? But what *were* they interested in? They weren't dancing, or playing games, or jacking each other off—not as far as I could tell from my bound position. It became easier, after a while, to believe that this roomful of horny boys posed no threat. But the atmosphere changed as the music changed. As much as I loved Black men, I'd never been able to unlock the secrets of hip-hop—couldn't tell one song from another. Then a favorite came on, and approving murmurs rose from around the room. Hands were clapping as I sensed a certain sweet, familiar smoke drifting through the air. The kids were smoking dope.

A tall kid with shaggy blond hair and an enormous dick walked up and looked me in the eye. "Did you say something?" he asked.

This was the first time I had been looked at so frankly and directly, having known only passing glances before, and it shook me. Maybe I *had* spoken aloud. My voice was still quite hoarse but I was able to say, "You guys are smoking dope. Is that allowed?"

"Oh, yeah." He didn't even blink. "This is the only time it *is* allowed."

"What do you mean, the only time...?"

He raised his hands and waved his long fingers to show how supple they were. "Torture time."

I cringed, as far as my restraints would let me. My fragile

sense of safety was shattered. "Please let me go."

"To hell with that." He reached toward another boy who passed him a blunt. It was uncommonly long and thick, like his dick, and he brought it down toward my lips. "We're gonna get you fucked up. Then we're gonna tickle the shit out of you."

I was writhing, I couldn't help it. "No...please...."

He was holding the joint at my mouth. "Shut up and inhale."

I did as I was told. There was a chance the pot would calm me down; it sure as hell couldn't hurt. Maybe I could even relax a moment before the torture began. But I was kidding myself. The first toke seemed to leap past my lungs directly into my nervous system, shaking me right down to my bones. "Whoa," I said, more unsure than before if I was speaking aloud. "I don't think I'd better...." I was still living in the past, far in the past when I still had a choice about anything. The blunt returned, or maybe it was a different one, held by a different hand. I inhaled, and suddenly the music was much louder, my senses as sharp as if I'd just leaped from a plane and was counting off seconds till I had to open my chute. Except I couldn't count or focus on anything for more than an instant. Apprehension, a sense of things happening or about to happen, began to spin me out of control. Dope-induced paranoia was familiar enough, but in a situation where I had been feeling paranoid *anyway* the new sensation was just unbearable. Now the table I was tied to was turning, slowly, uprooting itself from the floor, floating toward the ceiling, turning one more time so that I faced downward, not only bound by straps but hanging from them as well, hanging on for dear life, on the verge of bursting out into space. I was struggling and groaning, tossing myself back and forth as far as the restraints would allow.

The music was louder than ever, but I couldn't see anyone.

Where were the boys, the boys with the hard-ons, the boys who were going to put their hands on me…? I saw figures in the distance, blurry, wreathed in smoke, and I wanted, needed to *see* them. I wanted to read the intent on their faces, the malice in their eyes. I needed to size up their strength—to calculate, insofar as my fucked-up mind would allow, whether I'd be able to survive their attack. That shaggy-haired blond with the big red dick—how casual he'd seemed, his look opaque, as if my situation meant no more to him than the fate of a wadded-up newspaper in the gutter. Take his attitude and multiply it by…how many of them were there? Thirty, forty, sixty? Cutting their eyes toward each other, toward me and away, cruel thoughts collecting in them like semen in their balls, dirty boys, horny boys….

I loved boys. Had always loved boys.

The physical side of it started, really started, when I was sixteen. I was in the bedroom of Kyle Adams, a boy a year older than me who lived on my street. He went to a different school and I didn't know much more about him than that, except he lived on my street and just hung out in the neighborhood during the summer. While the rest of us went about our routines of summer jobs and chores and boring cookouts with our families, Kyle lurked at the edges, kicking a stone down the street or stretching out on somebody's lawn, staring at the clouds. Always, always with his shirt off. Was he really that tan, or was his skin just naturally of a slightly darker shade? Were his eyes green or hazel? How would it feel to run my hands over his hairy chest? I asked myself these questions, sometimes quite consciously, alone in my room, blushing in front of no one but myself as I slid my underwear down and beat off, daring to picture what Kyle would look like naked.

I avoided him like the plague.

Until the day I was coming home from the Bun-and-Burger, where I'd had to work a double shift, and was tired and aching and wondering how in *hell* a job that was so physically demanding could be so *boring as shit* at the same time. Was there anything on the whole goddamn planet that could keep me from quitting the next fucking day? Walking down my street from the bus stop, stripping off the skinny black tie they made me wear, I spotted Kyle, doing nothing as usual, leaning against a tree, his arms crossed on the naked chest that fascinated me so. He was wearing shorts, the cutoff jeans that showed his thighs, and he was *looking* at me.

I didn't care. I was hot, tired, and disgusted. I ran a hand through my hair, knowing I looked like hell, and a moment of despair stopped me dead in my tracks. I didn't know, maybe never would know if I was attractive to other guys. Christ, it was so much more than I could deal with at the moment that I could hardly lift my feet. When I looked up again he was still there. Had my thoughts, my horny obsessiveness finally driven me crazy, or was he looking at me as if…?

"Hey," he said, putting me out of one agony and causing a new kind of pain as I wondered what in the hell he could possibly want from me.

"Hey yourself," I said. How snotty did that sound? I tried not to care.

He came walking toward me. I kept moving but more slowly than ever, it didn't take him long to catch up. "Let's go to my place and smoke a joint," he said, as if he offered that invitation every day at about this time.

I stared at him till his half-naked form seemed to waver. I could feel the heat from his body, the sun his skin had soaked up. "Sure," I said. I was expected home for dinner, had never smoked a joint or even a cigarette in my life, had never before even spoken to a boy I was physically attracted to. Was I crazy?

I got my answer in Kyle's bedroom, on the top floor of a house down by the beach. It was hot, so hot that we peeled off all our clothes with no discussion. He lit a joint, pressed it between my trembling fingers, and taught me how to inhale. The smoke was so harsh I thought my lungs had caught fire, but that was nothing compared to the fire in my midsection. I had no doubt about what was going to happen, I could only wonder what it was going to feel like. As the smoke did its work that question grew more urgent, the entire surface of my skin felt as hard as my cock. Nothing would ease the pressure but his hands on me, and my hands on him.

Kyle was a natural. As easily as he taught me how to inhale he taught me everything I needed to know. We did things I'd never dreamed of, his hands guiding me smoothly through different postures of give-and-take, awakening every cell of my body. Lying spread-eagle on his bed with his tongue up my ass, I knew that from now on I was going to do everything I could with other male bodies—lots of them, more than I could fit into a sexual imagination that was expanding by the second, moving into new territory, adding new rooms and fixtures, mirrors on the ceilings, thick rugs on the floors.

He took me in his mouth. I came so hard I lost my breath. Then he told me how much he liked my *feet*. Like so much that he said and did, I didn't know what to make of this. I just let him handle me, picking up my feet at the ankles and rubbing the soles against his pubes. "Are you ticklish?" he asked, and I was so dazed that I didn't know what to say. Yes, it tickled, having my feet rubbed against his hairy crotch, but not enough to make me laugh or squirm. That happened when he started tickling my feet with his fingers, and I tried to pull them away, which only made him pursue them more. They wanted to fly, my feet, like birds trapped indoors, so he had to secure them tightly with my narrow black tie in order to tickle them as much as he wanted, while I shouted and cried and collapsed into alternate fits of hysterical giggling and desperate panting. I remembered the day I had witnessed the neighborhood kids tickling Old Man Abernathy, and how, unable to contain my excitement, I'd beat off in his kitchen. The combination of that memory and the tickling Kyle was giving me now made me moan and turn my hips side to side, surrendering to a lust I'd never felt before. When I looked I saw that my dick, fully erect again, had strands of what I would learn to call precum leading from its head to my pubes, and I said something like "Oh, my dick, it's leaking."

"The drooling dick," Kyle said, grinning. "I'll make it drool, all right. Make it drool for *hours*."

Just when I thought he'd tickled me to death, his fingers started exploring up my legs to my thighs and groin. He tickled my belly till I felt feverish with laughter, then explored my ribs and armpits. Part of me didn't want him to stop, and part of me knew that he *had* to stop, I couldn't take it. Struggling and panting, I got as far as the edge of the bed, then onto the floor. But that was no escape, it only made it easier for him to pin me in different positions and tickle me while I fought for the breath to beg him to stop. When he finally took a break it was to give my super-hard cock the pumping it so desperately needed. When I shot my load it was even more intense than before; I nearly passed out. Kyle raised his hands and spread my cum all over his hairy chest. Exhausted as I was, the sight of that got me on top of him, licking and sucking at that dripping chest hair, moving down to his cock, which I sucked for the first time—clumsily, inexpertly. I would get better at sucking his cock, much better; but he would always say that first time was the best.

So it was Kyle who taught me that there were boys like these, the ones circulating around the room as the music got louder and the smoke got thicker and I heard words like *cosquillas* and *chatouillement* and *solletico* and *cocegas* and a hundred variants. They were boys who, at one time or another, had felt the helplessness of a ticklish victim under their fingertips, and were now maniacs for inflicting that helplessness whenever and wherever they could, wanting to see how far, how deep it could go.

They were still mostly ignoring me, and it was making me more and more nervous. It stood to reason, in my panicky, stoned mind, that the less attention they paid to me now, the *more* attention they'd pay later on…or soon, very soon.

"Hey," I called out, tentatively. Then, "Hey!"

Murmuring, louder now, but still distant.

"Hey, somebody! Somebody come here." I was still writhing, I couldn't help it. Tossing atop the table, pulling on the restraints, thrusting my pelvis, I felt my dick growing heavy. Getting hard. Soon they'd be all around me, boys with big dicks and gleaming eyes.

Someone appeared at my side. At first I thought it was the blond kid who had spoken to me before, but this one was slightly different, a little darker and shorter. Christ, how some of them looked just alike, with their smooth faces and choppy haircuts.

"What do you want?" the kid asked.

"Please." It was all I could say. He would have to figure out what it meant, I couldn't say any more. "Please."

A few more boys drifted over. Excited young dicks raised their heads like dogs sniffing the breeze, even if the boys who owned them looked bored, standing with their arms crossed over their chests. Cutting their eyes at each other. A few more came over. Soon they were all around the table. Someone fitted a blindfold on me.

"Please," I said. Would it be a relief not to see those stoned, glittering young eyes? Could the darkness be any worse?

A lazy Southern voice drawled, "What the fuck do you *want*?"

"I...I...." In my poor stoned state I didn't know what I wanted. To be let go, of course. But if that wasn't going to happen—and it *wasn't*—then what else could I ask for? Something reasonable, something they'd be willing to do. *Please go easy on me.* How would that sound to a bunch of adolescent boys? I pressed my lips together, hard, to make sure I wouldn't say anything at all.

"I want his feet," another voice said. "Who else wants feet?"

There was a general shuffling around the table. Several voices spoke up. One might have been Japanese. Bare feet squeaked lightly on the hardwood floor.

"I want his ribs. I'm gonna *barbecue* those ribs, man!"

I was squirming again.

"I want his belly. That's my specialty."

"Oh shit, don't let motherfucking Davis work on his belly button. He'll be dead in two minutes."

"Hey Scott, what did you do with the tools?"

"Over here." A grunt, then something heavy sliding across the floor. "One big motherfucking bag of tools." It unbuckled and unzipped, rustled and clattered.

"I got his pits."

"Not all to *yourself*, you don't!"

"All I want are those balls." I could almost hear this boy, who had a Cockney accent, lick his lips. "Those big, juicy balls that look like they're ready to burst."

[77]

"Please please please." By now I was whispering. I was afraid to have them hear me, but I couldn't stop saying it, so I whispered. "Please please please...."

"You think he's got those sweet spots on his sides? That's what did the last guy in."

"I bet it's the thighs on this one. I can't wait to *squeeze* 'em."

"Shit, just give me some feathers and let me work on his neck for a while."

"Pleasepleaseplease." I was writhing even more, which they probably liked to see, but I couldn't help it.

"This guy's going nuts," someone said, "and we haven't even touched him yet."

"It's great, though," someone else said. Like me, he was whispering. "Just *talking* about what we're gonna do is driving him apeshit."

"You mean, like, working between his toes?"

"Feathering his dickhead?"

"Cotton swabs in his nostrils...?"

"How about the hairbrush on his feet? The one with the *hard* bristles?"

My body was on fire. They were as good as tickling me, only this was even worse because they were working together, their words and my own mind.

"Lotion up those feet. Get the soles nice and slick."

"I'm takin' his ribs, along with Callahan," a deep voice said. "I got stronger fingers than any a you guys."

"Yeah? We'll *see* who's got the strongest fingers!"

"Okay, we'll have a contest. A rib-tickling contest!"

"*And* a foot-tickling contest!"

"And the winner gets...what?"

"What the hell do you think? He gets to keep tickling for as long as he wants."

"Fuck! We'll do that anyway!"

All the words, all the threats, implied and otherwise, were working on me. A drop of sweat rolled down my ribs, and…I couldn't help it any longer…I laughed. Just softly, but once I started giggling I couldn't stop.

"Listen to this guy! Is he psyched out, or what?"

"We haven't even fucking *touched* him yet!"

"Wait'll we do, man." Another deep, intense voice. "Wait'll we do. He'll be screaming like he never screamed in his whole fucking life."

I twisted my head as far as I could to either side. More than giggling, I was flat-out laughing now. I couldn't help it. The more I tried to stop, the more I laughed.

"He likes hearing us talk, look at that fat ol' dick."

It was true, my dick—my big, stupid dick—was as hard as it had ever been, its head slapping against my belly as I tried to struggle.

"Wonder how many of us can tickle that dick at the same time. It's pretty big."

"Man, take a feather to that piss-slit and *work* it…."

I was laughing, a full-throated laughter that would not stop, that would rise and rise until I had laughed myself weak and could no longer struggle against the ropes. That was the horror of it: my laughter was making me more vulnerable. My own laughter was killing me.

The boys talked on but I could tell they were growing restless; they were all pent-up energy and horniness, and it would have to come out. Soon their voices were all blending together under the sound of my own laughter, until they all seemed to be chanting in unison:

[79]

Get him
Get him
Get him
Get him
Get him

When it came, it was like the belly-clenching moment when the rollercoaster car starts to plunge. Only it didn't stop.

4. DUKE

When the boys were through, the men in gray coveralls put me in a room by myself.

I didn't know this at first. I couldn't open my eyes, and my ears were still ringing with the shouts of boys and my own screaming. For hours sensation had seared me, rendering me fit for nothing but howling and tearing at my restraints.

I slept, and when I woke I did open my eyes. The room had three cots in it, a table and two chairs, and a counter with a sink, a small refrigerator, and a microwave. The yellow walls and orange scoop chairs reminded me of an employee break room in some outpost of industry. To come back from the ride I'd been on—and the coming back was a miracle, I knew that much—to a room as plain and dumb as this one struck me as hilarious. "They've got to be fucking kidding me," I said out loud, in a voice that squeaked and croaked.

I opened the refrigerator and found plastic bottles of water and juice. My hands were still trembling, and the tomato juice was almost too heavy to lift. Once I got a grip on it, my knees started to go. I'd moved too quickly, stood up too fast, and now I sank to the floor. I lay on my back on the linoleum, staring at the strip of fluorescent lights overhead.

The room, the cots, the refrigerator, even the tomato juice— somehow it was all *familiar*. I had been in this room before. As soon as I got up the strength, I stood and pulled open a door that was painted the same yellow as the wall, right down to the doorknob. Inside, a toilet and sink and shower stall, which I knew would be there.

I drank the tomato juice, and from a bowl on a table I took an apple. I sat in one of the chairs, but it wasn't comfortable enough to ease my aching ribs, so I perched on the edge of a cot. Now I could see something I hadn't noticed before, on the counter next to the refrigerator: a feather duster, of all things—a ridiculous feather duster with a white plastic handle. The feathers looked synthetic, dyed an orange color that lived nowhere in nature.

My memory had it this way: I had been brought to this place in the morning. First I had been turned over to the children, then the men and women had taken charge of me, then the horny teenaged boys. Then I had been pushed into this room. It wasn't a room I had been in earlier that day, yet I had been here before. Therefore, this wasn't my first day here.

How long had it been? A few days? A week? A month?

It was hard to keep thoughts together. Very carefully I stretched out on the cot and closed my eyes.

Next thing I knew the door was being unlocked. A wave of dread swept over me: they were coming for me again. But as I raised my head a young Black man was pushed into the room, the door shutting swiftly behind him. He crumpled to the floor, twitching and moaning, his arms and legs trembling. When he rolled onto his back, I saw the whites of his eyes under his half-open eyelids. His lips were swollen and parched, and he made a sound like heavy breathing or panting, which I soon recognized as laughter—the almost silent, insane, unstoppable laughter of a man who had been mercilessly tickled by many hands for a very long time.

I regarded my new cellmate with fascination and pity. I *knew* there had to be other captives at the Compound; one victim would never be enough for this crowd. But I couldn't recall seeing another captive or sharing a room with one. Of course they took no risk in throwing us in together: even three or four of us wouldn't have the collective strength to cause trouble. I could barely stand up, and this new man couldn't do even that. Naked like me, covered with sweat and cum, he might have just been released from the same gang of teenaged boys who had worked me over.

When I seemed to have enough strength, I sat up, slowly, and swung my legs over the side of the cot. I walked—baby steps, but at least it was walking—to the sink and filled a paper cup with cool water. I tried to carry it to my cellmate without spilling any, but my hand still trembled and I lost a few drops.

"Here," I said, lowering myself painfully to the floor. "Here's some water."

I might as well have been talking to myself; he was still in a deep delirium. Getting back on my feet was as difficult as squatting down but I managed it, then stood there holding the cup of water, not knowing what to do. Would his helpless whispered laughter ever stop? Finally I couldn't look at his tortured expression any longer. I tilted the cup and poured water down onto his face.

That jolted him, brought his dark eyes into view. They scanned the room, and his relief was so great to find that he wasn't being tickled anymore that he let his head fall back to the floor, untwisted his tangled legs, and began slowly waving his arms up and down, like a kid making snow angels. I knew how he felt: the red marks from the wrist restraints were still vivid, and it was so good to be free.

"I'll get you some more water." I filled the cup again, and as I brought it back he seemed to comprehend me for the first time. He took the water in his trembling right hand, gulped it down, and raised the cup, his eyes asking for more.

When I came back he was in a sitting position, looking at me with questions he couldn't find words for. He drank, wiped his lips with the back of his hand, and managed to ask, "How long you been here?"

I shook my head. "I've been trying to figure that out myself, just now. I was thinking I'd only been here a day—one incredibly long day—but now I think it's been longer."

"Oh, man." His voice was still little more than a broken whisper. "I think I've been here a long time, too, but I ain't sure anymore. My mind"—he made a few circles with his index finger at his temple—"it comes and goes. You know?"

"I know. What's your name? I'm Rand."

"Duke." Wincing, he raised a huge hand. The hand shook but his grip was strong. He had the build of a tight end, which hadn't saved him from having to learn the hard way that strength was no defense against ticklishness.

"How did you get here?" I asked.

He shook his head sadly. "Dude named Granger."

"*Granger*?" It was the first time I'd heard that name spoken by anyone else.

He continued to shake his head. "Oh, yeah. I saw his ad. Thought about it for weeks. I didn't know what to do, but every time I pictured…what he said he'd do, my dick would just about bust through my shorts."

"I was the same way."

He looked up at me as if I didn't understand. "No, you see… it started with my sisters. My two older sisters. All my life, while I was growing up, they used to tickle the shit out of me."

"Well, I never had sisters or brothers," I said, "but I guess you're bound to be tormented sooner or later, if you're real ticklish."

"Ticklish? Shit! I'm *more* than ticklish." He was still shaking his head as he talked, and I wondered if he had gone through his whole life that way, looking down, shaking his head. "I'm fuckin' *disabled*, that's how ticklish I am. Didn't take my sisters long to find out, either. See, they used to babysit for me. My folks would be going out all the time, and the minute we were alone Brenda and Janessa would have me down on the floor—stripped *naked*, man, they didn't give a shit—and start ticklin' me all over and never stop, no matter how much I screamed and shouted."

As if it had heard its name, his dick twitched a little. I tried not to look, or at least not to be obvious about it. But the more I glanced at his long, smooth, circumcised dick, the more I wanted it. I ran my hand across my mouth and stepped back, feeling my own much-abused dick start to tingle.

"When I grew up, and Brenda moved away from home, then it was just Janessa. Then it was Janessa and her boyfriend Duane. She got him into it *big* time. Sunday afternoons they used to tie me to their bed and tickle me for hours. All three of us naked. Sometimes Janessa would jack me off, like both my sisters always used to do, but that Duane, he liked a little more than that. He'd get on top of me, suck my dick while he's tickling my ribs, and Janessa at the foot of the bed tickling my feet. Sometimes she'd tickle Duane's feet too. Man, Janessa tickling Duane's feet, telling him to tickle me harder if he wanted her to stop, and he's digging into my ribs and suckin' my dick, the three of us tremblin' and shakin'...shakin' like we're about to *blow*."

By now I couldn't hide my erect prick. I *knew* that deadly passion for being tickled, and could picture those three beautiful Black people whipping themselves into a frenzy. Exhausted as he was, Duke's prick was getting hard too, curving up from his groin; so I wasn't totally ashamed to say, softly, "Sounds hot."

His eyes looked off as he shook his head. "Hot? Shit! It was so hot I don't know why we didn't fuckin' *melt*."

"Sheer torture, but it turned you on anyway."

"Oh, hell yeah." He reached down and stroked his dick, just once, like giving minimal attention to a showoff pet. "But Janessa and Duane split up a few years ago, and she moved away and he got into some other shit…so I knew what to do when I saw Granger's ad. My *dick* told me what to do."

I didn't want to think about Granger or the events of the past… few days? A week? Two weeks? Instead I let myself look at Duke, naked, spread out at my feet. He was quite hairy, a thick pelt spread across his pecs. His beard and mustache were overgrown, but if I squinted I could see how he must have worn them once, trimmed close, setting off his lips.

Raising a hand to my chin, I discovered that I had a beard too. When had I last seen myself? Had it been a few days? A week? A month? I had no idea. Somewhere even in that stupid, sterile room there should have been a reflection, some surface to give me back at least a part of myself. I checked the tiny bathroom again to make sure: no mirror. Nothing on the counter, either, except the blank dark face of the microwave. I was turning back toward Duke, ready to try to find some way to ask him how I looked, when we heard it.

It was a scream. A scream that ripped my spine out and packed ice in its place. As we stared at each other, Duke's mouth sagged, his face lengthened into a melancholy look that seemed, weirdly, to suit him, and his voice deepened with despair.

"They're gonna tickle us to death, man," he said.

All the strength bled from my knees, and instead of helping him up I was sinking, sinking to the floor by his side, my head spinning. "Wait," I said. "Wait, wait…."

His eyes rolled in panic. "Oh, man, we're gonna die."

"Shut up. Shut up for a minute." I was as scared as he was, but talking about it would only make it worse. "We're not gonna die. We can get out of here."

Duke shook his head. There were tears in his eyes. "Shows how much you know. Ain't you seen the guards?"

"I haven't seen anything but grinning faces and hands."

"Well, you'll see." He raised himself onto his elbows so he could look at me without straining his neck. "I'm not talking about the guys in the gray outfits. They're—what you call it?—trusties. I'm talking about the dudes in camouflage. With rifles, man. As if that fence wasn't enough, with all that razor wire shit along the top."

I saw what Duke described, dim memories surfacing. Barbs of razor wire against a blue summer sky. "Don't," I told him. "Don't talk about that stuff."

"Man, don't let 'em catch you." He blinked, looked around the room as if there was some menace lurking even here. "We shouldn't even be talking like this."

As much as his paranoia fed my own, it also made me angry. I swatted at the air in frustration. "We're already fucking prisoners, what more could they do?"

"I'm telling you." With some effort his raised his head higher. "I ain't told you yet, but here it is. There was this dude who tried to escape, see—"

In my agitation I interrupted him again. "Who? Did you know him?"

"Naw, I just heard about him from this other guy I was put in with once, like I was just put in with you. Anyway, the dude tried to escape, and they caught him, those guys with the camouflage

[87]

and shit. They did the *worst* to him."

"What?" God Almighty, what could be worse than what we'd already suffered? I pictured bayonets tearing at flesh, a naked man shred to pieces.

He swallowed, hard. "They turned him over to Junior."

That name stirred some association in my fevered brain, but I couldn't quite place it. "Who's that?"

"Dred Junior," Duke said. "Sometimes they just call him Junior."

One drop of sweat trickled down my back. Dred Junior. *Junior.* "Jesus Christ."

"Man, once they put you in with that crazy fucker, nobody ever sees you again."

"Is he really crazy?"

Duke nodded, slowly. "They say he's kept in a straitjacket all the time, except when somebody's brought to him—down where he stays, in a cellar. He picks up where the rest of 'em leave off. It's that intense. And there's screaming like you never heard before."

If I weren't already on the floor I would have sunk to my knees. Even my stomach felt weak under the weight of what little I'd eaten. "How do you know all this?"

"That guy I was put in with that one time? Name of Franklin? Poor kid, he was only nineteen." Duke's voice, already weak, sank to a whisper. "He was *one of them.*"

"One of...?"

"He was one of the crackers. Just another farmboy, like the rest of them, except he must have done something really bad. They turned on him, made him one of us."

One of them. One of us. It was the language of war, of terror; and it was our language now, mine and Duke's, the only kind of talk that made sense here. But war and terror also meant strategy.

"Maybe this kid Franklin was just a plant," I said. "Maybe they were trying to psych you out by putting him in with you."

"Naw, man. He wasn't no plant."

"How do you know?"

"'Cause he died. He *died*, man. That's all I can tell you."

We sat in silence for a few minutes. Duke looked as miserable as I felt, but we had moved close enough for my bare leg to touch his. Even in these bizarre circumstances I was grateful for the intimacy; and I thought of how, in another life, Duke and I might have been close. Suddenly I wanted to stretch out next to him, feel his length all along me....

He looked up at me again and swallowed hard, and I was ashamed for letting my thoughts drift like that. Duke had been here longer than me, had been tortured more than me. He was a wreck.

"I want to ask you something," he said now. His *ask* sounded like *ax*.

"What is it?"

"I'm dead serious, man. Believe me?"

"Why shouldn't I?"

He swallowed again, as if words kept getting caught in this throat. Finally he said, "I want you to do it."

"Do what?" Even as I asked, my spine went cold again. "What are you talking about?"

He didn't speak till he was sure my eyes were meeting his. "I want you to do it," he said again, but this time he spread his arms, just slightly, revealing more of his tender sides, his ribs, his armpits—leaving no doubt about what he was asking. "Tickle me to death, man."

I jumped as if he'd thrown off fire. "Jesus Christ!"

He stirred, agitated by panic and need. "Do it, man," he said.

[89]

"Do it! I'm half-dead already, and I'd rather have you finish me off than those motherfuckers out there."

"Chrissakes, you don't know what you're saying." Still shaky, I got to my feet. It was urgent, very urgent that I put some distance between us and, at least for now, not even look at him.

"I *do* know what I'm saying. You're different from those sons of bitches."

"Well, then, how can you ask…?"

"You could do it…as a kindness."

I had to look at him then. "Torture is torture, Duke. It's cruel either way."

"No, it ain't." His eyes were begging. "Listen to me. There's a place…they all know about it, even the little kids. That's the spot that'll kill me someday. But you could do it now. Put me out of my fucking misery."

"You're talking crazy."

"But don't you *see?* They keep damn *near* killing me, time after time, but they let me live so they can torture me some more. *Help me,* man!"

No one with a heart could ignore his desperation. Still I turned away. "No. I can't do it."

More silence. For the first time I wished I'd never laid eyes on Duke. I sat on the edge of my cot—how revolting, *my* cot, as if I belonged here, as if anything in this place was mine—and stared at the floor. Finally I said, "You should get some rest. Grab one of these cots." I stretched out and closed my eyes, hoping for a few moments of oblivion before they came for me again.

"You could do it," he said.

I didn't open my eyes. "Don't bother me."

"I know you could. Because *I* could. I *did.*"

I looked at him then, but he had turned his head, as if in

shame. "What did you do?" I asked.

"That kid, Franklin. I tickled him to death."

"Bullshit!"

"No, man. I *had* to do it. He begged me." He turned his eyes toward mine, and they were too sad, too genuine to doubt. "They were going to turn him over to Dred Junior. He couldn't stand the thought of it. It was driving him fucking crazy."

"Jesus Christ, Duke."

"I used my nails on his soles till they bled."

"Oh, Christ." I didn't know if Duke meant it was the kid's feet or his own fingernails that had bled. I didn't *want* to know.

"Please," Duke said. "I'm begging you, just like he begged me." Though it was difficult, maybe even painful, Duke rolled over on his side and reached out, as if he were only asking me to help him up. "They know, man. They know I killed Franklin. They ain't said anything, but God help me, I think they might turn me over to Junior. I can't take it!"

I turned to face the wall, wishing the cot had a blanket I could pull up over my head. "I've got enough to think about now to give me nightmares for the rest of my life. Thanks a whole fucking lot."

Silence. Then Duke mumbled something like "Okay," and the subject was closed. My eyes were closed, too, and I was trying to clear my mind, to think of nothing, when he spoke again.

"Oh, I get it," he said.

"Get some rest, for Christ's sake."

"You don't like Black."

"*What?*" Amid all the horror and disgust and fear, I was surprised to find anger surfacing again.

"You don't want to help a Black man." A sneer in his voice now. "You're just another cracker."

I rolled over and stretched out my arm, aiming a warning finger at him. "You don't want to be saying that. Really, you don't."

"Why not? It's the damn truth, *cracker*!"

I raised my admonishing finger and rubbed my temple with it. It wasn't good, the way my blood was stirring. "You really, really don't want to be saying this."

"One more nigger in trouble, one more point for whitey."

"God *damn* it!" Tired as I was, it was enough to get me on my feet again. "You don't know what the fuck you're talking about. I'm crazy about Black guys. I'm fucking *helpless* about them. Always have been." Seeing that sneer on his lips, I got down on the floor again, right by his side. "And you, you're...."

"What? Say it!"

"You're...beautiful." I reached out then—I had to touch him, had to. Very lightly I grazed his side with my fingertip.

His whole body quivered. In a different, desperate voice he cried out: "Oh shit, don't do that!"

"Sorry." Yet I couldn't keep from touching him again, in just the same way. I loved the look of it, my white fingers against the deep, deep color of his skin. Again he shook, and he wasn't putting it on: he really was that ticklish. With both hands I tickled along either side of his navel, and he erupted into full-fledged giggles that rose in pitch as my fingers played all over his hard abs.

"I get it now," I told him. "You were just baiting me, weren't you? You were trying to get me mad, so I would tickle you. Admit it!"

"No! Naw man, no...!"

"*Admit it!*" I moved my fingers to his groin, where his beautiful black cock was lengthening, thickening as I tickled on either side of it, down to his balls, to his inner thighs. "You were trying to get me mad on purpose!"

He was laughing so hard he couldn't speak, but shook his head in denial. It made me furious, but even in my angered state I was getting turned on as well. I had never tickled a man before, not like this. I watched, as if from afar, as I crawled down the floor towards his feet.

"No, man!" It was all he could do to speak. "Not my feet!"

"*Yes*, your feet, motherfucker!" I lay atop his legs and gave my fingernails the run of his soles. The effect was immediate: I felt the jolts going through him as he gave in to full-throated laughter. After about a minute of this, I twisted around to look at his face. "Are you gonna admit now that you made me mad on purpose?"

Panting, he shook his head "No."

"Okay then." I got up, went to the small bathroom, took a washcloth and moistened it under the tap. When I returned he was still panting from the last attack. "You were laughing a little too loud, my friend," I told him as I stuffed the cloth into his mouth. "This will take care of that."

He resisted, but soon enough I had stuffed the cloth completely into his mouth as his eyes widened with fear. When I turned back to his feet again I was moaning from both anger and lust. I *wanted* his black feet, more than I'd ever wanted anything in my life. I attacked his soles with my fingertips again while I used my tongue on his toes. Soon I had them in my mouth, sucking on each one as if my life depended on it. The smell of his feet, a smell that was both clean and sweaty, drove me mad.

Duke was too weak to struggle, too weak to even try to take the gag from his mouth. But he was shaking all over from his stifled laughter, his hands flopping uselessly on the floor. As I stepped up the intensity, licking and even biting his soles, his muffled laughter turned to screaming.

"You haven't felt anything yet," I said. The transformation was now complete, I had become someone else, a crazy man with a hard dick and fingers itching for wild, sustained tickling. My thighs trembled as I straddled his thighs, my fingers reaching deep, deep into his armpits. "I'll tickle you the way your sisters tickled you. The way your sister and her boyfriend tickled you, when you were tied up and helpless. They weren't *crackers*, were they?"

Tears ran down his cheeks as I buried my fingers deep in his pits, the flesh searing hot, the tightly coiled hairs teasing the ticklishness of my own fingertips as I worked them hard. Panic filled his eyes, panic that grew as his muffled screams grew in volume and he could do nothing more than sway weakly back and forth, like a rocking chair losing its momentum.

"And what about *me*, Duke? You want to be put out of your misery, but who's going to help me? I ought to just keep tickling you, man, just like they do—tickling you to death, only *not quite*. Over and over, never stopping…."

His face was a mask of fear and agony. The gag distending his cheeks made him look even more grotesque. It got even worse as I moved my hands down a bit, toward his upper ribs. His fingers stretched and spread, they would do anything to stop me, but he couldn't even lift his hands from the floor. Yet his dick was hard, yearning toward his belly.

"You *will* move those hands," I told him. "You're going to bring yourself off. Or else."

I kept tickling his ribs as his weak, trembling right hand found his dick. Grasping it seemed to take extreme effort.

"I remember what you told me. There's one spot that'll kill

you. But I'm not even trying yet. You're going to come first."

He shook his head violently.

"Do it! Come on!"

Slowly his hand began to pump his cock. To get a better view I moved down, down…to his feet. He couldn't even clench his toes as I attacked his soles again, but through the gag he gave a little *yelp* of panic and started jacking faster. The more I tickled his feet, which were now so helpless they couldn't move at all while I dug my nails into the soles, the faster he jacked himself off. As I watched him I saw all the other Black men I had known in my life. Lustrous dark skin in streetlight leaking through a pulled shade, or glistening in the dimness of a bathhouse room. Smooth curved dicks with heads brown, pink, or purple, swollen and ripe. Nipples clinging to a curve of muscle or hiding in coarse, tight curls. Navels like darker secrets within darkness.

Amid Duke's muffled laughter and grunts of exertion as he worked his cock, I heard another sound and realized I was whimpering, whimpering and whining like a dog as I relived twenty years of desire and torment. And it was with a cry like a wounded dog that I left Duke's feet and leaped toward the counter next to the fridge, grabbed up the ridiculous feather duster and leaped back at him, furiously tickling his balls as he came, his thick cream rising and falling to glaze his hands.

I was crying. Crying from exhaustion and madness. I rested my head on Duke's thigh, felt half of my face sticking to him, my fingers still roaming that crotch that reeked of a lifetime's worth of sweat and cum. When I finally unstuck my face and looked up at him, he was the same as when I'd first seen him, his head twitching, his eyes unfocused and half-closed.

"Okay, Duke," I told him. "I'll do it now, I promise. It should be easier now that you've come. Maybe quicker, too." I wiped my face with my forearm, trying to clear away tears and snot. "I don't guess you need this now," I said, pulling the washcloth from his mouth. "Just tell me the spot. Tell me where to go."

I waited. It would take a while, my words rattling through his tortured consciousness, before he'd be able to give me a sign. When it came, it wasn't his lips that moved but his arms, spreading slowly, bracketing his ribs. "Is that it, Duke? Somewhere on your ribs?" I thought I saw a flicker of assent in his nearly sightless eyes, but again it was his body that spoke, jolting as if a current passed through it when I probed his upper ribs, gradually increasing pressure.

By now he was as helpless as a slab of meat on a butcher block, but he was still *living* meat, my fingers sending shocks through his system that were no less intense for his inability to make a sound. The merest twitch, the slightest tug at the corner of his mouth told me I was getting to him. I lay my head on his stomach, my ear pressing into cold sweat and cum as I pushed deeper, deeper into his ribcage, deeper into a man's body than I'd ever gone, seeking more than the mere connection between skin and nerve: it was the secret of life itself I was after, its hidden link to the soul. I burrowed toward it like a man buried alive clawing through dirt.

"This is it, Duke." My teeth were clenched against the work I had to do, my fingers ached from pressing and twisting, but I couldn't stop. It would all be over, any second now.

When I finally did stop, it was because I had learned to listen to his body so well. True, it pulsed in agony, sent to hell by my tickling; but was I really taking him to the end? My mind raced over the brief time we'd spent together. When he'd accused me of bigotry he hadn't meant it; he was trying to goad me into attacking him. Having broken that code, what did I have to unscramble *now* to understand what he needed? Nearly slipping on my sweaty palms, I heaved myself up to a sitting position. "It's not your ribs after all, is it, Duke? You couldn't quite bring yourself to tell me what that spot is…that fatal spot. You need me to find it myself." His breath was hoarse. Soon it would be a death rattle. "Soon, soon," I promised, touching his dry lips with my fingertip. "I'm going down to your feet again, Duke."

His labored breath came more quickly as I stroked his soles, but I had to try something I hadn't tried yet. I reached for the feather duster one last time and pulled out one of the larger, stiffer feathers. Holding his foot in my hand, I guided the feather in between the big and second toes—a spot I hadn't reached before, not in this cruel way.

It rocked him as nothing else had. His feet came to life, struggling and flexing with surprising strength, desperate to protect the pink spaces between those slender toes. It didn't matter. I put an armlock on his ankles and went to work. With his toes clenched I could still tickle his soles; he couldn't flex them enough to totally escape my fingers. Scraping with my nails into the arches, around the heels, back toward the center of the soles, I felt I'd regained some of my old strength. I really could do it: I could tickle this man to death. "I'm not going to leave your feet, Duke," I said through clenched teeth. "I'm going to keep tickling them, no matter what, till you let me get between those toes again."

His burst of strength was fading. "That's better," I said as his feet began to relax, through no will of his own. "You know I'm going to get them, Duke. I'm getting between those toes. And that'll be the end of you." Soon enough I was doing it, working that big stiff feather into those tender crevices, twisting and pushing and pulling for maximum effect. He was weakening,

weakening, and I didn't know if I would ever be able to stop, even when it was finally all over for him.

"All right, that's enough!"

They burst in on us, half a dozen of them or more.

These weren't trusties but the serious ones, the guards, in their camos and combat boots. They cussed as they moved over us, pulling me off Duke, dragging me to the opposite corner of the room. Kneeling around the body of the Black man, asking each other, "Is he dead?" and one of them answering, "Naw, he ain't dead. Not quite."

Once they heard that Duke was still alive, the men holding me down started tickling me furiously, their practiced fingers nearly tearing my ribcage apart. "So, you want to tickle somebody to death, huh? *Huh?*" Their taunting wasn't necessary, my screaming laughter and the tears streaming down my cheeks were proof that their tickling was destroying me—as if Duke's ordeal, my merciless treatment of him, had made *me* even more ticklish.

Soon my feet were captured, fingers prying my toes back, exposing my soles to more fingers. The tickling short-circuited my brain. I couldn't think of anything beyond begging them to stop as soon as I could draw a breath; but I was aware that they must have been watching Duke and me all the time. And from my vantage point as I lay on the floor with my head thrown back, I could see even through my tears a surveillance camera high in one corner of the room, something that anyone whose brains hadn't been scrambled would have noticed much sooner.

Yes, I had broken Duke's code, found my way to the core of him; but breaking the code of this hellish place was more than any one tortured soul could manage.

11. MY NAME IS M-36

I. DRED JUNIOR

The guards dragged me to another building, into a room where rows of benches faced a small stage. On the stage was a narrow, elevated platform, with a set of ankle stocks at its end. They shoved me, still naked, face down onto the platform. I continued to tremble all over from the tickling they'd given me in the break room.

They locked my ankles in the stocks and, holding my arms against my sides, began to fasten leather bindings around me, the first wrapping around my shoulders, the next around my upper arms, just a few inches down from the first. These thick belts continued all the way down to my calves, and because I didn't know any better, not yet, I was grateful that they covered so much of me. Most of my ticklish spots were now out of reach, except for my feet. Thank God, they were only going to be able to tickle my feet! That I was so fully bound, so incapable of moving even a fingertip, was frightening in itself; yet I was so glad that they couldn't tickle my armpits, ribs, belly, and thighs anymore that I was close to crying from happiness. Even the platform I was belted to was my friend, its padded surface cool against my cheek. That was a fleeting pleasure, however, because soon hands appeared to raise my chin and fit it into a kind of soft brace that made it impossible for me to turn my head any longer, or to look down.

I faced a blank screen, like a computer monitor. After a few moments of staring I realized the screen wasn't blank after all.

It was showing me something, I just couldn't tell what. A barren landscape, maybe—a wide stretch of tundra, pale frosted earth with the mere shadow of a seam here and there, a suggestion of texture. I stared long and hard at this picture till it disappeared, as if my eyes had devoured it.

Now the screen darkened and filled with color. The colors separated into images that were somehow familiar, though I had never seen them from this angle. This was the videotape, the secret recording they had made of what had happened between Duke and me. There I was on the floor, bent over him, tickling for all I was worth. How had I found such energy, my fingers darting all over that beautiful helpless body as if I were having fits? His panting and weak, weak laughter seemed so clear now, much clearer than when I was part of the scene, concentrating on my work.

"No, man!" I heard him yell. "Not my feet!"

The monitor screen went blank again, or rather returned to its earlier state of not-blankness, its view of the pale tundra—a landscape that supported no life, yet was itself strangely alive. Of course I knew what was on that screen: it was no landscape, but human skin, a surface that meant more to me than the crust of the earth. I had always lived on skin, made it my home, the rest of the physical world an uninteresting given. So I wasn't that shocked when the zoom lens pulled back, slowly, revealing that I'd been staring at the center of the sole of my own foot. My right foot. As the lens moved again I saw the entire sole, then the soles of both of my feet.

For a minute, maybe two minutes, maybe five, I stared at the screen. In spite of my bound position, my inability to move a single muscle, I was wriggling. Writhing from my shoulders right down to my trapped ankles. It wasn't a physical motion but a mental, emotional one, a stirring of panic through every inch of my being. Soon it unhinged my tongue as well.

"Please let me go," I said. "Please. I don't even care if I get my clothes back, just let me go. I won't tell anybody about this place, I swear to God, not anybody, for the rest of my life." Fear kept jarring my voice; I tried to keep it low and steady but it was fluctuating wildly, rising at odd places, exactly as if...oh God, as if I were *laughing*.

"I could help you," I said, fighting desperately to control my rising hysteria. "I could find other guys for you, I could bring them here. I could! Lots of ticklish guys...."

I shouldn't have been surprised when the sensations first shot from my soles to my head, but I was surprised. That was the continuing astonishment of it all: that even though my body had been overstimulated to the nth degree, the tickling felt new every time. My brain could recall in excruciating detail the tortures I'd endured, but my sensitive skin had no memory at all and was freshly affronted by each assault, my outraged laughter testifying to my vulnerability and helplessness. The irony now was that they weren't really tickling me—that is, what they were doing did not have the primary purpose of tickling me. They were binding my toes.

This was the most cruel bondage of all, for while it didn't tickle my wrists to have them bound, and it didn't tickle my ankles—not too much, anyway—to have something wrapped around them, it was agony to have my toes individually tied. Michael Loomis, the madman who had abducted me and brought me to the Compound, had found this out to his delight as he'd forced binding rings over my toes, making me scream with laughter; and now I was finding it out all over again as my toes were meticulously spread and tied with something just soft enough, just rough enough to coax maddening sensations from the creases and crevices where my foot-flesh was as smooth and white as fresh snow. By the time they finished my left foot I was begging them to leave my right foot alone. Amazingly, they did. But this was part of the torture, for as a minute passed with no one touching my right foot, the *anticipation* of what was going to happen became unbearable. "Oh please please please," I was saying, "please please please." They knew, they must have known, that I was both begging them to tickle me and begging them not to.

I was almost at the breaking point when they finally, slowly began to bind the toes on my right foot. My head was spinning again, spinning toward and away from the hateful thought that the real torture hadn't even begun. On the monitor I could see, through the tears in my eyes, each piece of cord being wrapped around each toe and hooked into place against the stocks. It was an ingenious arrangement, my feet angled away from each other, the heels much closer together than the toes, giving free access to my sensitive arches.

I couldn't see the room behind me, but I could hear the crowd jostling the wooden benches that rocked and squeaked against the floor; and while I couldn't make out anything they were saying, I could tell that there were men *and* women *and* children, perhaps every single resident of the Compound filling that space. If I knew this bizarre group by now, they all had their favorite tickling tools with them. And they had fingers that itched to scrabble against a man's most sensitive flesh, and ears that hungered for hysterical laughter and screams and pleading.

And they were all facing my naked feet.

My feet…how still they were, as if the monitor were showing me a photograph or painting rather than a live image. I couldn't twitch a single toe, couldn't give myself a sign that these were, in fact, my feet. So there was, if not exactly hope, perhaps a possibility that they *weren't* my feet. "Those aren't my feet," I said now, as if I could expand possibility into fact. Maybe if I talked enough. "Those aren't my feet on that screen, I know they're not mine, whatever you're going to do, going to do to them, they aren't mine, they're not my feet...." Overcome by hysteria, it was all I could do to get the words out between bursts of high-pitched giggling. On and on I went, my insane spirits rising to a peak of triumph, of exaltation. "You can't touch my feet!" I crowed. "Ha ha, you want to touch them but you can't! You can't touch me!"

By the time I paused long enough to be able to hear anything but my own voice, the crowd had quieted except for a few scattered coughs or the occasional squeal of a child—enough to reveal that they were still there, ganged up behind me, settling into an anticipatory hush. I raised my head as far as I could—maybe an inch—and cried, "They're not my feet!"

A hand settled on the crown of my head and eased it down till my chin touched the support again. It was almost soothing, that hand, firm but gentle, warm against the cold sweat of my scalp. But its insistent pressure was also a warning, a signal that I mustn't raise my head even an inch, must keep my eyes level, because something was about to happen on the screen and I had to see it.

For a few seconds there was nothing new to see. The immobilized feet, pale and glowing under the lights. Feet that were being warmed, or "roasted," by flames held just out of sight, not close enough to burn the flesh but enough to tenderize it, and to summon a thin layer of sweat that would make each touch a lingering torment. Then a flicker appeared at the bottom left of the picture, like a speck of dust or lint flashing briefly across the lens. It appeared again, slightly larger, lasting slightly longer this time; and I watched as I had never watched anything in my life before, not a screen nor horizon nor distant street corner. *Was there something there, or not?*

Just when I had convinced myself that I was only imagining that dark flickering, my eyes grown tired and untrustworthy, it came again, a little larger, a little more clearly. But what was it? Was it some kind of *creature* in the frame? Did claws or fur cast those threatening sharp shadows? No...the shape was unmistakable enough as it grew larger, clearer. No amount of madness could disprove its existence or deny what it was.

A feather.

"Oh, no...." A voice completely given in, surrendered to misery. *Not my voice. Not my feet.* And then the first touch, the briefest swipe, across the center of the sole...briefer than a blink, yet foretelling entire worlds of sensation—multiple histories, stretching over eons, of what I had first thought was a landscape but was really a universe.

As my screams rose in pitch—*not my voice, not my screams—* the crowd responded in kind, calling out for more.

More, more, more!

Forever, forever, forever!

***

I woke up in a room that was totally bare except for the white blanket I was wrapped in and a small hard pillow. I had been bathed, at some point; I had slept, for how long I couldn't say; and I had been fed, for my stomach wasn't small and hard with hunger but felt normal, as if I still led a life. I was glad to find that I could stand up, though my legs wobbled a bit. I could even stretch my limbs gently without aggravating too much the muscular aches and pains that were a chronic feature of life at the Compound. Yes, I felt rather normal, all over.

But that was the last I would know of *normal*, for as soon as the doorknob rattled, accompanied by the sharp sound of an opening deadbolt lock, I hurled myself onto the blanket and wrapped up into a tight ball. I had developed the reflexes of a ticklish animal driven mad by its captors. *"Don't,"* I said as the men appeared—two of them, not guards but trusties, judging by their gray coveralls.

One stopped just short of me, thoughtfully stroking his red beard. "We've come to take you," he said. "It's time."

"Time for what?" My head snapped from one to the other.

"You know you broke the rules, M-36."

"Don't call me that!"

"Your name is M-36." It was the tall one speaking now, one I remembered because of his piercing blue eyes and deep black beard. I remembered what he was called here, too: T-49. In my former life I would have found him attractive. Incredibly, once I might have *asked* him to tickle me.

"I don't think he remembers," the redhead said.

"What? What's to remember?" My voice was as clipped and abrupt as my movements.

"Let's get going," T-49 said. "This is dangerous work."

"Jesus Christ," I said, "don't tell me you guys are *afraid* of anything."

"No, he doesn't remember," the redhead said. He looked at me with what might have been a trace of pity, and held out his hand. "Maybe it's just as well. Come on, let's go."

I rolled myself up even more tightly. "Go where?"

T-49 spoke again. "Stop wasting time, for Chrissakes."

With the blanket fallen away I was naked. They placed me on a gurney and fastened straps that bound my arms to my sides. I began to squirm with panic.

"Take it easy," T-49 said, nothing calming or reassuring in his tone.

Soon we were moving down a bright corridor. I glimpsed plain white walls on either side of me, strips of fluorescent lighting overhead. Gone were the shabby, rough-hewn surroundings I'd grown used to, walls of splintered barnboard, plain concrete floors. "Tell me where you're taking me," I said. "Please."

After a moment the redheaded one spoke. "You're going to your punishment."

"What? I already got my punishment! I sure as hell haven't forgotten. I not only felt it, I had to *watch* it on that monitor!"

The redhead mumbled something I couldn't make out. Then he spoke a little louder. "That wasn't your punishment."

"I was strapped to a bench, for Christ's sake. I watched every stroke of what was done to my feet...."

He said again, "That wasn't your punishment."

A wave of dread passed over me as I began to understand what he was saying. "If that wasn't my punishment, then what the hell was it?"

"That was just part of the normal routine."

The normal routine. I began to laugh. Helpless laughter was all I had left as they rolled me along on soft rubber wheels. I laughed till my chest heaved painfully against its restraint and my head bobbed against the padded surface of the gurney. Fresh tears pooled in my eyes, distorting the strict order of the overhead lights. They had almost killed me...had certainly driven me mad...and *now* they were going to *punish* me?

T-49, who walked down by my feet, looked back at his partner and asked, "What did you tell him?"

"Nothing. I just said he was on his way to his punishment. I guess that struck him as funny, considering what he's already been through."

This raised a smirk on his partner's dark, cruel features. "Huh. Well, when you think about it, it is pretty fuckin' funny." He had turned around so he was walking backwards, and without warning stretched wriggling fingers toward my feet. They were relatively free, my feet—held down by a strap across my ankles, which was nothing like the toe-bound constriction they had so recently known; but by now they'd been tickled to such sensitivity that I could barely stand to have them exposed to the air, let alone to a sadist's hands. Helpless with fear, it was all I could do to pull in enough breath to shout, "Don't! Don't tickle my feet!"

My new tormentor raised his chin toward his partner, and the gurney slowly rolled to a stop. "What the hell," he said, "we've got a few minutes." He reached for my feet again, as I begged him not to. That made him laugh. "It cracks me up," he said, "the way they keep begging, even though they know it's no damn use."

Like an idiot I tried to reason with him. "You've been a victim too," I said, "both you guys have, you've been through this yourselves, how could you do it to someone else? How?" Before I could say more his hands were all over my feet. The look on his face added to my hysteria. I had seen that look before. I had *sought it out* before, in my fantasies and on the face of Granger, who had told me, over a computer and by phone, exactly what he wanted to do to me. And I had told him, slavishly, that my ticklish body would be his to do with as he wished. I'd lie awake at night picturing his cock getting hard, just as T-49's was now, the fabric of his coverall bulging. He tugged at the zipper pull at his neck, exposing his hairy chest and belly and setting his cock free, a cock that wanted my feet as much as his hands did. His wet dickhead stroked and poked my soles, rubbed against my toes. When he found he couldn't manipulate my feet freely enough, he undid the ankle restraint, which allowed him to grab my ankles and bury my sweaty, precummed soles in his groin, use them to scrub his heavy balls and caress his cock. I didn't think the tickling could get any worse, but it did as he sank to his knees and let his tongue, teeth and beard do what they wanted.

"Hey," the redhead said, "guy's got a boner a foot long."

It was true. There was a direct connection between my feet and my dick. Tormented as I was, I couldn't keep from getting hard. Neither could the redhead. Before I knew it he was standing at the end of the gurney too, his coverall unzipped, and he was banging his cock into my left foot as T-49 banged my right. It seemed to last forever but they stopped short of coming, instead sticking their engorged dicks back into their coveralls.

I wondered later if that attack had been planned all along. The delirium it produced certainly added to my fear and confusion. When we were finally moving down the corridor again I was still laughing and begging, in a voice that had once again been reduced to a pathetic croak. Even when I understood that they were no longer tickling my feet, I sensed the friction of the gurney's rubber wheels against the tile floor, I heard the *clop, clop* of the men's boots moving in unison, and it was as if those pressures and sounds were working on my skin, which was now part of the surroundings, the walls and ceilings and floors, stimulated and stroked by whatever moved on or through it.

It was a miracle I could collect the words to ask, once more, where they were taking me. "We're taking you to the bad place," the redhead said. "The less you know about it, the better."

Was it my feverish mind, or was the corridor gradually growing darker, the lights dimmer and farther apart? With some effort I focused on the walls on either side of me, and saw how they had become darker too, no longer white and smooth but shadowy and grainy, like stone. At the same time the air we passed through, caressing and stroking and playing at the edges of my ticklish skin, had grown cooler. Dampness and must worked into my nostrils as my mind raced to determine what this place reminded me of; and as we descended further—I could sense the floor slanting down, the men shortening their steps to keep control of the gurney—I knew exactly what I was feeling. It was the chill of a cellar.

I could hear poor Duke, who had lived in mortal fear of being taken to Dred Junior: *They say he's kept in a straitjacket all the time, except when somebody's brought to him—down where he stays, in a cellar.*

"No!" I shouted, loud enough to echo off the stone walls.

"Looks like you finally got it," the redhead said. "Listen."

I had a lot of begging and pleading to do—who had time to listen? Still I held my tongue, kept my ears tuned beyond the near-silent wheels of the gurney and the clip-clop of boots to hear ...what was it? An unnatural, unearthly, yet all too familiar sound. Laughter—demented male laughter, deepening, rising, separating into more than one voice. Piped-in sounds of torture designed to make my ride along the last mile even more terrifying. Weakened, my head buzzing, I recognized some of the laughter as my own.

The overhead lights were gone, replaced by pale flickering sconces. I could just make out a row of elongated shapes set into the walls. "What...what are those?" I asked.

This time the redhead didn't answer, as if the walls could

speak for themselves. My teeth began to chatter, from cold or fear or both, as I realized I was looking at grave markers. The corridor had become a crypt.

When the gurney stopped I cried out. The men unbuckled the straps holding me down. I was so afraid of what would come next that the feeling of being released was worse than being bound. The men were solemn as they took my arms and got me on my feet in an efficient, practiced manner. "Please," I croaked. "Please, no." The recorded laughter had stopped—another blessing that was more like a curse, since I could now hear my own panicked breathing and whimpering echoing off the walls.

Holding me firmly by my upper arms, the two men led me to a door with a small barred window. I could sense *their* fear of what lay beyond.

"Make sure," T-49 said. "Make sure as shit he ain't already in there."

Both men peered anxiously through the barred window, then searched their pockets hurriedly. T-49 found the keys to the deadbolt locks above the knob.

"Hurry up," the redhead said.

They opened the door and shoved me in as if they were feeding me to a wild animal. The locks snapped shut behind me, and I heard the two men who had brought me running away, their footsteps fading down the corridor. I was on the floor of the cell, on my hands and knees; as hard as they had thrown me I wasn't hurt because the floor was padded. It took a supreme effort to get to my feet, but it had to be done. I wanted to be standing, to have what little control that would offer as I faced whatever was coming to me. As my eyes grew accustomed to the light from the single, barred window high above, I could see that the walls were also covered with slick gray padding, no doubt serving several purposes—protecting the abused from broken bones, muffling screams, and allowing for quick cleanup of any spilled body fluids. I could also see that I was alone; I considered, briefly, that the scope of my punishment might begin and end right here, as a solitary prisoner in a padded cell. There would be no more torture, except for the torments of solitude.

That fleeting hope, bleak as it was, vanished as a scraping sound issued from the padding on the far wall. I could barely make out that the padding was pieced together there, sectioned in a way that allowed a door to open, a small square door no larger than what would be needed to shove a wild animal through. From the strange groans and growls that came through that opening, I judged that it might in fact be a wild animal, and I was about to be eaten alive. And it was a creature that was shoved through that door—a foul, hairy creature the size of a small ape, hauling itself to a spot where the faint light would allow it to examine me. More groaning, more growling, and as the whites of its eyes flashed I could see it was human, after all—a short, wiry man, the upper part of his body wrapped in something. Staring, I realized he was wearing a straitjacket, and it gave every sign of being tightly fastened. *This* was the ultimate threat? A little man with useless arms? Not so long ago I would have been calm, certain of my advantage in this situation; but in my weakened and fearful state I could only feel my legs going out from under me. Soon I was sitting and hugging my knees, my back against the padded wall, watching the creature across from me, not daring to close my eyes or even blink. He sat with his knees drawn up also, mirroring my position, and was still for so long that I began to wonder if I were somehow *projecting* him. As if he could read my thoughts, he spread his knees slowly, revealing that he was naked from the waist down. I saw his erection, the pale shaft seeming to collect enough light to actually *glow*. And for the first time I heard his words: *Helpless. Hopeless. Doomed.*

Yes, they were his words, but where had they come from? His voice—if it was a voice—wasn't issuing from that far corner of the cell. It seemed closer, much closer. I remembered what Duke had told me, why the thought of being taken to Dred Junior terrified him so: "He gets *inside your head*, man." If I had doubted that statement, Dred's next words made me a believer.

Yes, he said, or thought. *I'm speaking from inside your mind.*

I made a noise, a little yelp; and I thought, This is it. I've gone completely mad.

He smiled, like a tight-lipped ventriloquist making his dummy sing. *No, you haven't gone mad. Not yet, anyway.*

I tried to move, but my arms and hands were too feeble to push against the padded floor. If he really was receiving my thoughts then I was flooding him with pleas and promises, begging him to leave me alone. If only I could reason with him, connect with him in some way—

Suddenly my thoughts were shattered by a blinding flash of light, though I was pretty sure that, as far as the physical world was concerned, no light had flashed. Christ, what was happening to me?

It hasn't even begun to happen yet, he thought. *But it will. Soon.*

Squinting at his face, searching out something more than his tangled hair and the whites of his eyes—something more human—I wondered if I would get out of that cell alive.

Alive? Maybe. But forever changed.

Trembling more than ever, I begged him to let me go. I begged like a creature with no heart or mind, nothing but a nervous system on the brink of snapping. Letting go of my knees, I sank sideways onto the cold soft floor, ignoring the cries of my aching muscles as I stretched and writhed.

For a while it's fun to watch you beg, but then it gets boring because there's no use in it. No use at all.

But I know you, I thought. *You're Dred Junior, the little brother that Jason and Josh had, before Michael came. I've suffered some of the things you've suffered. You're not insane, you know right from wrong....*

Another flash, and I instinctively blinked against an aftervision that was not really there. Now even my thoughts were reduced to abject whimpering. *When will you start, when is it going to start, when, when...?* I blinked, wondering if those blinding flashes had altered my vision. Had he moved, had he actually come closer? No, try as I might I couldn't see that he'd moved a hair; he was still squatting across the cell from me, his erection exposed. Was I safe as long as there was distance between us?

That was when he laughed, this creature, this Dred Junior, and his mind spoke the words he'd been saving up for me: *It's already started.*

I was still lying on my side, in a fetal position that would, I knew, protect me from nothing. But I pretended, feverishly, that I couldn't feel a thing. *Nothing can touch me, nothing can harm me.* In spite of my claims my feet were tingling—just lightly at first, then more intensely. I straightened my legs, stared at my feet. Nothing was touching them! Yet the sensations along my soles were unbearable. I bit my lip and flexed my feet till they were nearly bent double. I rolled and pounded my fists against the padding. Finally I let go a stream of nearly breathless, hysterical laughter.

Make it stop, I begged. *Oh God make it stop...!*

Now he tickled the entire surface of my feet—tops, soles, between the toes—with full abandon, till they were on fire. I screamed, kicked, rolled across the floor. With energy I didn't know I had I leaped up onto those fiercely tormented feet and stomped them as if I could put the fire out. I lunged from one side of the cell to the other, laughing, crying, hurling myself against the gray walls.

You see, came his words, *the padding isn't to protect me. It's for my visitors.*

You're fucking killing me!

Intense, isn't it? What do you think would happen if it spread…over your entire body?

I stopped breathing, and wasn't sure I would ever start again. But soon enough I was gasping. While the tickling stayed at my feet—I could feel it even under my toenails—I felt a tingling in my armpits too. Wrapping my arms around myself did no good. I ran again, back and forth, as the tingling spread downward from my armpits to my ribcage. I was fighting the soft walls, fighting for my life. Fighting myself, finally, struggling for some focus as I stopped my useless running and tried to concentrate on my tormentor. Having never killed in my life, I was ready to kill now. It was beyond the question of right or wrong: it was my life or his. I ran straight at him and lunged, hungering for his filthy neck.

I hit the wall. Bouncing back, disoriented, I whirled around and saw him now against the wall on my right. I lunged again, with a strength that was rapidly waning, and again I missed—or rather, he had vanished, only to appear against the far wall, beneath the barred window. I chased him once more, though it was agonizingly clear he was only a vision, an image, nothing I could get my hands on, nothing that could be stopped. I staggered, slipping in my own sweat, and landed on my ass in the center of the cell.

Okay, no more running now. You'll pass out from exhaustion, and I won't let you have that luxury yet. In fact, I'd rather you didn't move at all.

Tickling began between my legs. First my scrotum, my balls lifted and tickled, then the underside of my hard dick. A wicked tickling finger slid up my asshole. My titillated nerve-ends had taken over and were fast becoming all that would be left of me. I raised my head—which took all my will with my neck being tickled—and screamed at him, calling him every name I knew.

You're still thrashing around too much. I'm going to have to hold you still. Here....

I raised my head once more and saw him, crouched in the same position as always, that obscene erection springing up between his hairy thighs, the whites of his eyes glowing. With the sleeves of the straitjacket still fastened around him, he raised two ghostly hands, palms facing me, fingers absolutely still, mocking the thousand tickling sensations that wracked my body. He shifted the hands deftly, like a magician...and a second pair of hands appeared, right next to the first. A twist of the wrists, and they revealed...a third pair of hands. Now four, six, twelve pairs of hands, reaching toward me on snakelike arms, bobbing and weaving across the cell. Of course I was still laughing, screaming, and pleading for him to stop; but something else overtook me as well, a kind of hilarity—because this was...oh, God... this was *funny.*

Now? I thought. *Now you need hands? You were doing pretty fucking well without them!*

Oh, I don't really need them, he said. *But you have to admit, they make a great visual!*

And so they did, all of those hands crawling through the air, holding me down so I could do nothing but lie still and be tickle-tortured till the end of time.

2. THE CHAMBER

Once you've misplaced the difference between sleeping and waking, it's hard to find it again. I spent a long time in the gray area between the two—long enough for time itself to become an insufficient measure, a teaspoon shoveling a beach. It was only because I could dream that I knew I was still alive, even though the dreams were all the same, with slight variations, my dreamlife reduced to one channel.

It would begin like this: I'd wake up in a cell, with nothing to see except three bare walls and the yellow bars facing a brightly lit hallway. The light over my head, a bare bulb hanging from the ceiling, was bright also, and I kept blinking, wondering why there should be so much light when there was so little to see.

Sitting up on the edge of my cot, I would find I was naked as usual. My body, which I had done without for many unconscious hours, was a thing of fascination for me. Strong calves and thighs, well-equipped loins, a tightly muscled chest with a smattering of black fur—it all hardly seemed to belong to me, as if I had borrowed it, like a suit, and forgot I had put it on till I happened to look down. Though I was clearly in a prison of some kind, it didn't look like a prisoner's body to me—or rather, it looked like prisoners' bodies in TV shows and movies: well nourished, well exercised, and full of malevolent energy. It took me a while to get caught up with this physical presence. Usually I'd start by wiggling my toes. They were long, those toes, but not skinny, and as I wiggled them I was acutely aware of the ticklish spaces between them. The soles of my feet were also ultrasensitive; I couldn't keep them on the cold gray floor for very long.

I would be lying down again when I heard footsteps in the hallway. Of course I was curious to see who was coming, and yet full of dread, too—not because I had anything to fear, but because I was afraid that I knew who was coming, and confirming it would rob the moment of its novelty, the prick of curiosity that was another sign I was truly alive. *Alive*, I thought, knowing my life was valuable, and my active consciousness was the most precious thing in the world and I had to do what I could to protect it. I couldn't say *why* it was precious, since it didn't have much to do beyond monitoring my surroundings, taking note of the temperature, the light, the sound of the approaching footsteps, and the hospital smell of rubbing alcohol and floor wax drifting in from the hallway; yet there was a kind of buoyancy, too, in my state of mind. Something like *hope* seemed to be jumping up and down inside me, seeking my attention.

Of course it was Crystal who appeared at my cell door. I placed her so quickly that I was able to meet her "Good morning, M-36" with a "Good morning, Crystal" without missing a beat. I smiled, thinking how surprised she would be to know how disoriented I had been just a few seconds ago. Or would she?

Crystal opened the cell door and I stepped out into the hallway, completely unself-conscious about my nakedness. I didn't try to hide my genitals, and wasn't afraid to brush lightly against her as I passed and she turned to lock the cell door again. I led the way down the hall, which surprised me because I couldn't say where we were going, only that this was familiar—as familiar as Crystal herself, with her long, coppery hair and the white slacks and smock that made her look like a nurse.

We passed no other cells, just smooth white walls leading to a swinging door at the end of the corridor. Through that door was another corridor exactly like the first, but I found my steps speeding up, my breath quickening as if I knew where I was going and couldn't wait to get there.

"Slow down, M-36," Crystal said, her footsteps as unhurried as when she had come to get me. She seemed self-absorbed, her eyes fixed on the floor just ahead of her, and I noted how strange this walk was compared to others I had taken. I wasn't shackled or strapped to a gurney or dragged by the arms. Our walk together as two human beings was almost *normal*, except that I was naked and she was one of my captors.

I turned a corner without hesitating, as sure of my path as if I followed these walls, these bright fluorescent lights every day. Maybe I did. I wasn't sure, though, till I pushed through the last double doors and saw the Plexiglas cell—the Chamber— and the chair with the wrist and ankle restraints and the paraphernalia surrounding it: machines with dials and switches, electronic probes that were now at rest. I was whimpering with anticipation, like a dog whose food bowl is being filled, so that Crystal had to speak to me again: "Calm down, now, this will just take a minute." She disappeared, leaving me on the outside of the Chamber while she went to get the key. I stood in place, forcing myself to take long, deep breaths; my heart was still racing when she reappeared with the key, a plastic card, and slipped it into the slot near the Chamber door.

In a few seconds I was in the chair. Sitting back activated the restraints, adjusting perfectly to my ankles and wrists as headphones slid over my ears. Held tight as I was, I sensed the suppleness of the chair, the ease with which my limbs could be manipulated, and knew that I was more free strapped into that device, more capable of receiving pleasure, than if I were totally unbound. Still without knowing exactly what was going to happen next, I began whimpering again, and salivating too so that I had to keep swallowing. Crystal was at my side, unscrewing the lid of a small brown bottle, then holding it under my nose. One sniff and the potent, sweet-scented fumes hit my brain. Now I was moaning, the sounds amplified and broadcast back to me through the headphones. My cock stiffened to its fullest, and my eyes rolled back in my head. Crystal attached the device that hugged my dick as closely as the restraints held my wrists and ankles. "Please," I was begging. "Please, please." Something was going to begin, something *had* to begin or I would burst.

The gentle humming, the vibrating sensations came none too soon. Electronic fingers gently cradled my scrotum, and now my moans were constant as my balls were ever so gently teased and tickled and stroked and the vibrating sleeve made love to my cock. The chair spread my legs wider, more fingers moving in to explore my asshole and manipulate my prostate. I could see all of this happening without lifting my head, courtesy of an angled mirror suspended over my midsection. I could not see my feet, so it was a shock when my toes were encircled by something that seemed to flow between them and then become rigid, holding them perfectly still. Aware of the implications of toe bondage, a momentary panic flashed through me; but I was so engulfed by erotic sensations that I could not have moved those toes if they had been free. Sure enough, in a few seconds two more unknown mechanisms cradled my feet, and an intense, blunt pressure began to travel up the center of each sole from heel to toes, then back again, over and over. Unlike the unbearable, agonizing tickling I had known most often, this was deep and devastating in an erotic way that made my cock strain against the vibrating sleeve that alternately teased and satisfied its complex longings. And instead of moaning, my voice was now rising to a high register, a sharply pitched *keening* in the headphones, stunning and strange, like the song of an exotic bird. There would be no more surprises, headed as I was toward the inevitable. Each stroke of my extended soles fed the erotic fire consuming me, sparking all the secret places where tickling excited pure lust. I could die from this, or be replaced by it, my longing for orgasm taking on a form more real than my body.

At last my entire being shot through my cock.

Perhaps Crystal was a nurse, after all. She took me back to my cell, wheeling me on a gurney only because I was trembling too much to walk, and produced a hypodermic.

"This will help you calm down," she said. "After all, you have to go to work soon."

Sure enough, my gray coverall, the uniform of a trusty, was laid out on the bed.

3. T-49

On a typical day, my partner and I might start work by greeting a new arrival. It was like standing on the opposite side of a mirror as I watched the blue panel truck eat up the road that led to the wide front lawn. Michael Loomis would get out—as flustered and agitated as ever, his muscular body well-defined by the wifebeater he wore—and open the passenger's side door and dump a burlap bag onto the grass. Out of the bag would fall a half-naked, wild-eyed man, trembling and twitching, his breath coming in short, shallow gasps, his hands clawing the ground weakly. My partner and I would grab him under the arms. He'd be terrified of touch but too weak to do anything but pant; we'd have no trouble dragging him over to the schoolyard, where the kids would play games on his ticklish skin.

My work partner was none other than T-49, the tall, black-bearded sadist who had helped transport me to my meeting with Dred Junior, of which I remembered nothing. I had no hard feelings toward T-49; he'd been doing his job, just as he was doing it now, with me beside him. I called him T, he called me M, though we worked mostly in silence.

We took one victim, who had been at the Compound several days, to the stocks in what I thought of as the village square, where I had first been tickled by the men and women. He had been in those stocks before, and he begged us to let him go. He was sure they were going to tickle him to death this time. T had little patience, as usual. "You come along quietly," he said, "or we'll just take you to Dred Junior right now."

The victim settled down. He had been there long enough to know that being taken to Dred Junior was the ultimate punishment. We fixed his trembling limbs in place and watched as the men and women circled around him. Within a few seconds he was hysterical and screaming.

Occasionally we had a victim who was able to walk by himself, like one young man we had to take to the teenaged boys' party. A big bear of a guy, he moved along silently, refusing to beg or show any fear. The boys, already half-stoned by the time we got there, were overjoyed, reaching out for him before he was properly tied down. As more and more of them gathered around him he looked at me and said, through clenched teeth, "They're gonna kill me."

"Take it easy," I said. I had learned how to talk like a trusty, never conveying any comfort or reassurance. What else could I do—pretend that the air in that room wasn't stifling with hormones and desperation?

For such a big man, his screams of laughter were surprisingly shrill.

Another man who had been tickled for several hours needed to be taken to a break room. When we released him from the table he had been tied to he jumped up so quickly that T lost his balance and sat down hard on the floor. Somehow this one still had the energy to try to make a run for it, so before he could get completely out of reach I grabbed his ribcage and started tickling him. "Hey, help me, T," I said, and together we tickled his ribs and armpits till he sank to the floor.

"I want his feet," T said.

"Go for it," I said, quite used to T's insatiable appetite for feet. Now that we had weakened the victim I had no trouble pinning his upper body to the floor while T satisfied his needs. I was facing the wrong way to see what he was doing, but could tell from the expressions on the victim's face that T's lips, teeth, and tongue were *devouring* that tormented, ticklish flesh, and would not stop till the guy had passed out.

One victim did manage to break away from us. He was short and stocky but fast on his feet, and it was a workout chasing him across the Compound. Sheer panic kept him moving, but it proved to be his downfall: he ran blindly into a tickle torture session in the village square, and before he knew what was happening some of the men in the crowd had him pinned to the ground and were working him over. He was feather-sensitive to the *n*th degree, and the men had plenty of feathers to use on him. Where he had been running from us a few minutes before, he was now reaching out to T and me, begging us to save him. We were in no hurry to break up the party, since a line had formed and there were now men, women, and children waiting to tickle him. We stayed and watched till it was time for our next assignment.

Throughout all of this I felt nothing; I was just grateful to be left alone. At the end of the day Crystal would walk me, slowly and thoughtfully, to the Chamber, where I would get my sexual release again, powerful enough to clear my mind of any doubts and put me to sleep for the night.

***

The most difficult duty was taking a victim to Dred Junior. I remembered part of my journey to that underground chamber, including the part where my current partner had had his way with my feet. But what had happened when I finally reached Dred Junior wasn't clear to me. I couldn't picture how he had looked or what he had done. I only knew I'd made the transition from victim to trusty so successfully that I could view these tormented souls with little or no emotion; and when T-49 wanted to break the rules one day to take another detour on the way to Dred Junior, I could only shrug my assent.

The victim strapped to our gurney, a young man of Hispanic origin called S-73, was so scared he was hyperventilating, a steady stream of Spanish escaping softly from his lips like prayers from a deathbed. T, at the foot of the gurney, kept looking back over his shoulder and licking his lips, turned on by the young man's fear. We hadn't even reached the hallway where recently installed audio effects would begin—the overhead playback of screams and laughter, including the victim's own; nor had we reached the "tombs" with the inscribed list of all the men who had been tickled to death. But S-73 was twitching and panting and praying at such a rate that he was going to wear himself out before we got halfway there. That was when T said, "Let's take a detour." There was another young man with us, H-80, a new trusty who was catching on quickly. He had no problem with helping to maneuver the gurney through a set of swinging doors off to the right, into a side corridor.

I leaned over the victim. "S-73," I said, "you've got to calm the fuck down, man."

Could he even hear me? His eyes were rolling wildly, his muscular brown chest heaving. I reached out and gently took hold of his legs, just above the knees. That one touch galvanized him, his body leaping as if he were having a seizure. It was a tough body, right from the streets—a body that had kicked and fought and fucked and unleashed its relentless male energy in a thousand ways. His brown pecs and abs, arms and thighs bore a scar here and there, or a tattoo—like the primitive rose curling enticingly close to his right nipple and, more intriguingly, *REYES LATINOS* stenciled in large ornate letters across his abs. How was that possible? Wouldn't tattoo needles be torture to` a ticklish man's belly?

I let my fingers crawl across his thighs, feeling their strength and resiliency, the life pulsing just beneath the surface. As my fingers moved faster, tickling, kneading, squeezing and stroking, his whispered prayers and curses gave way to a bubbling stream of laughter. The sound was both odd and familiar—odd in its squealing, insane pitch, yet familiar because it was the kind of laugh that all the victims developed, having been tickled so much that they would never laugh normally again. Meanwhile T and H-80 were down at his size-12 feet, licking his soles and sucking his toes. I remembered very well having T's merciless tongue between my toes, and it made me shiver. Reaching up, I traced the letters on our victim's belly, *REYES LATINOS*, with one finger, making him yelp in ticklish panic. That a man so powerfully built could be so sensitive....

T had unzipped his coverall, his enormous cock swinging free at the foot of the gurney, so I unzipped mine too. H-80 followed suit. Obedient kid, he wouldn't do anything unless T and I did it first, but he was game, his hefty dick as hard as ours. I continued to spell *REYES LATINOS* over and over, tracing the ornate letters on skin that broke into a sweat, making my fingertips glide that much faster. T was fucking those strong brown feet, turned on by the long toes wriggling against his dick. He stopped, though, before he could shoot, and backed away. After a moment he tucked his hard dick carefully behind the zipper of his coveralls. I did the same, without knowing exactly why. I knew only that I got my sexual release in the Chamber, once every morning and once every night, and must have learned at some point that any sex play with the victims could only go so far.

H-80 stepped up. He was a strawberry-blond farmboy, indigenous to these Midwestern hills—unlike the Hispanic kid, who must have looked like an exotic piece of tail to the new trusty. Certainly that brown torso with its crude rose tattoo was a novelty, and H-80 grasped either side of the ribcage and set his fingertips loose to explore. Judging by the agonized expressions on S-73's face, it didn't take long to find the most tender spots. Mercilessly clinging to them, H-80 actually raised the victim's torso off the stretcher, *lifting* him by his ticklishness. S-73 arched his back and screamed, not at the top of his lungs but at the bottom, a hoarse, scraping sound of utter despondency. He was losing all strength, his hands useless, his fingers frozen in a curled, desperate shape. In another minute he would be nothing but pliant flesh.

I moved to the end of the gurney and studied those big sensitive feet. They had been tenderized by the Compound experience—scraped, scrubbed, beaten, and roasted into a permanently reddened and fragile state. I could *see* how ticklish that faintly glistening skin had become. I started eating those feet, slurping along the soles and between the toes. Their slightly salty taste tingled along my tongue, and they had the mysterious smell of reeds growing at the edge of a lake. I dug my thumbs into the ball of each foot, nibbled at the arches. He was panting again, frantically, his eyelids twitching, his mouth grinning grotesquely from ear to ear as the tip of his tongue swung to and fro like a bell clapper. Soon his panting became as silent as the drool leaking from each corner of his mouth. I wanted to take him even farther into the remote zone he had entered, to test the limits of where we both could go.

"Hey," T said, "Ease up. I don't like the looks of him."

I freed my cock again, let my dickhead probe among his toes, precum lubricating the way around and between them. I took hold of my throbbing shaft and whipped that dickhead against his soles. This was what Duke had wanted, what I'd tried to give him after he'd begged me to tickle him to death.

I didn't know how much time had passed when T suddenly threw himself at me, pinning me against the corridor wall. "You crazy fucking bastard, you've killed him!"

"No...impossible...."

I could protest, but it was true that if a body had ever looked lifeless, it was the one I stared at now: its head twisted to the side, mouth open, no movement in its chest or belly, no more panting, nothing. Yet just a moment before he'd been breathing…a moment before, a minute before…maybe two minutes, maybe five…how long *had* I been at his feet?

"You've done it, all right," H-80 said. "Shit! What do we do now?"

T's lips twisted into an ugly sneer. He looked me in the eye and said, "Dred's expecting a victim. We'd better bring him one."

The tone of his voice rattled my bones. "No," I said.

"Sorry, bud," T said, "but if it's gonna be one of us, it sure as hell won't be me." He turned his head to the side, toward H-80. "Come here and help me."

That was my chance, my only chance. I wheeled around and started running—not toward the main hallway we had come from, but deeper into that mysterious building, where there were more dimly lit corridors ahead. Close behind me came T's boots pounding the floor. I was running for my life but he was running just as fast, if not faster. A continuous row of fluorescent fixtures streamed past overhead, but only a few bulbs were working. We ran in and out of shadows, covering what seemed like a mile before we heard H-80's voice behind us.

[129]

"He's alive!" he yelled. "Hey! He's alive!"

I had no breath except for running, and precious little of that left, but I managed to yell over my shoulder at T, "Stop! He's alive!"

T kept running, I could almost feel his panting on my neck. The corridor we followed would soon end in a blank wall; I veered off to the left, into another corridor just as long. Here the few lights that worked were flickering, breaking up the stretches of darkness with eerie strobe effects.

"Stop!" I yelled again, my chest about to cave in. "T, stop!"

He was so close his words were practically in my ear: *"Like hell!"*

So it was up to me to stop—but not in a way that would let T get his hands on me. Without even looking I jumped off to the side, right into the corridor wall, which hit me like a fast-moving vehicle and threw me backward onto the floor. I felt bruised all over but the move had worked; unable to stop so quickly, T had run on some distance ahead and was just now turning to face me.

I was so out of breath that it hurt my lungs to talk, but I had to get some words out: "Stop…it's all right…didn't you hear… S-73's alive!"

"Yeah." Still striding toward me, he wiped his mouth with the back of his hand. "So what." He moved into a brighter patch of flickering light, and it was easy to see his huge cock straining upward against his coverall.

I held up my hand, palm outward. "Let's go back."

He sneered again, the ugly curl of his lips as expressive as the hard glint in his eye or the bulge in his crotch. "Ain't no going back now," he said.

I scrabbled, trying to get to my feet but only pushing myself backward in a kind of crabwalk till I hit something and fell. Hard but yielding surfaces met my skin. I had stumbled into a nest of boxes that were empty except for bits of styrofoam and brown wrapping paper. A soft but effective trap, tilting me on my butt with my boots off the floor, walls of cardboard rising steeply on either side of me.

"I've got you now," he said, panting, sweating from the chase, his hair hanging in limp curls. "I hope you're ready for what's coming to you."

"No...please! It's okay, don't you get it? I didn't tickle him to death."

"Who gives a shit?" His boots clapped the floor, not quickly as when he was running, but slowly, deliberately. "The only thing that matters is *your feet are mine!*"

It was a strain, but I could lean to my left just far enough to see behind T, down the corridor. "Look out behind you!"

Just briefly his sneer became a laugh. "You must think I'm fucking stupid."

"I'm not kidding, they're right behind you!"

"Every word you say is only making it worse for you, buddy...."

"Listen, you dumb prick, they've got cameras *everywhere*, you know that. Did you think they wouldn't come after us?"

"Oh, for Christ's sake." He twisted his head to look around. Throwing myself against the side of the box, I spilled out into the corridor. In the second it took him to turn back toward me I pushed some boxes into his path, then jumped to my feet. If panic had sped me before, I was practically flying now with the knowledge that if I stopped, my feet would be fucked to death or tickled to death, or both.

At the next break in the corridor I turned left. *Were* there cameras, even back here? It seemed to me there must have

[131]

been, or else the Compound would have sealed this building off completely, whatever it was. But another turn, this time to the right, brought me up to a dead end—a hole in the floor, a drop-off so wide I couldn't possibly jump over it. I couldn't even see, in the poor lighting, where the floor picked up again, if it did. Squinting into the dimness I saw only wreckage and ruin, suggestions of collapsed walls and ceilings, ducts and pipes and wires hanging twisted in the air, snapped apart like so many pieces of licorice. T's footsteps were behind me, a little heavier now, a little slower, but unstoppable. I could either jump *into* the void facing me, or—a grate in the wall next to me, some kind of air duct, was my only other choice. It was small, hardly big enough for me to fit through, but I had no time for second thoughts. Thank God two of the screws meant to hold the grid in place were missing, and I could quickly work the other two open with my thumbnail. The space was so small I had to keep my arms extended in front of me, working my hips and using what little purchase I could get with my fingertips to pull myself completely inside. My body heated up the aluminum duct immediately, I was like a potato baking in a foil wrapper.

"Come out of there, you son of a bitch!"

With no way for me to replace the grate, T had spotted my hiding place right away. He couldn't follow me, not with his broad shoulders, but that didn't help me much. I screamed in fear as his fingers clutched my bootheel. Like our coveralls, those boots had been made for quick removal, and one tug pulled my right one free. Then there was the thin white sock that he was grabbing at the toe and pulling, dragging the length of the sock across my ticklish sole. Then my left boot, my left sock. Even in this place my feet had never felt so naked. "T!" I cried out. "T! Can you hear me?"

"Save your breath, asshole. You're going to need it."

"Wait! Wait, wait! What about…the Chamber?" This was one of the shared areas of experience we never discussed: the Chamber where we got our sexual release. It seemed a safe assumption that it was as important to him as it was to me. "If you kill me, they'll kill you, and we'll never see the Chamber again." I pressed against the aluminum walls that offered me so little room, so little hope. The thought of never seeing the Chamber again did fill me with overwhelming sadness, and a tear mixed with sweat ran down my nose. "We've got to go back, T! We've got to go back!"

No reply—but he wasn't touching my feet, either. Thank God, he had heard me. I could *feel* him thinking, trying to reason it out, even with my helpless bare feet right in his face. Then it began— such a gentle stroking and caressing of my feet that it might have been a breeze passing over them. But if there had been a catch in my voice as I mentioned the Chamber, there was that same choke of emotion in his as he said, "I want these feet. I had them once, and I've been dreaming about them ever since. Even when I was sitting there, in that Chamber, it was these feet that I wanted. And I *will have them.*"

With that his fingers took on fire, and he growled with pleasure as he set them loose on my ticklish flesh. My panicked, nerve-racked state only intensified the torment, paralyzing me as I gasped and begged him to stop. Of course that made him tickle harder, his fingers scrabbling against my much-abused soles. Too weak to move, I felt all strength leaching from my arms and shoulders as I succumbed to helpless, suffocating laughter: I was going to be tickled to death after all, then abandoned in this aluminum-walled coffin. But the very thought of ending up that way, in such a humiliating grave, gave me one last ounce of strength. Somehow I began to move, hauling myself along with thrusts of my hips and thighs, my sweaty fingertips on the aluminum walls helping to move me forward far enough to finally drag my feet out of reach.

"God damn it!"

I panted, trying to shake off the sweat running into my eyes. I might never get the strength to move again, but at least I had found blessed relief.

Then, incredibly, the tickling started again, even worse. T couldn't reach my feet with his fingers, but he'd found something—a length of broken cable, maybe—to use as a tickling tool. What felt like a thousand jagged wires dragged over my soles, poked between my toes, making me completely helpless again. "Oh Jesus…oh don't… you're killing me this time…."

"Goddamn right I'm killing you! I just wish I could get my fucking *hands* on you!"

I could see, even in the darkness, a kind of sparkling at the edge of my vision, and knew I was on the verge of passing out. I was also shouting, in a demented voice that was totally unknown to me: "Go ahead, you bastard, tickle me to death!"

"Goddamn right I'll tickle you to death…!"

"*Ahhhhhh* I don't care anymore!" I broke the final law of sanity by forcing my feet open, unclenching my toes, letting the tickling wires do their work, and now I was singing, fitting a hysterical little tune to my words: "I don't care anymore, I don't care…!"

T was happy, oh he was a happy winner! He whipped that cable, or whatever it was, all over my feet and ankles while I yelled and laughed and sang and surrendered. My light-headedness only increased when I felt, even in the midst of torment and fear and exhaustion, my *dick* getting hard. Talk about funny! That omnipresent dick, that mindless fuckstick that had caused me so much trouble, asserting itself one last time…unbelievable!

Hilarious! To die with a stiff prick, what could be more fitting? Yet *fitting* it wasn't; there was no *room* to get properly hard, my dick being trapped between my belly and the floor of my coffin. I tried to suck in my gut so my dick would have room to swell, but there was no way, not while I was laughing and ranting and panting. Weakly I tried to turn or twist, anything to give my cock a little of the room it demanded. The more I tried, the harder it got, as if it enjoyed my desperate state and wanted to exploit it to the max. I sang a little song of pain, *Ow, ow, ow,* as I twisted and struggled, struggled and twisted, throwing my weight to either side over and over, anything to ease the throbbing that seemed bigger than I was. My vision began sparkling at the edges again, and soon I saw nothing but stars.

Sometime later—a second? a minute?— I became conscious, the darkness inside my head unfurling into the recently forgotten darkness of my prison. Two things were clear, even to my tortured, unhinged mind: number one, I wasn't being tickled anymore. Number two, my dick still throbbed and ached. And oh, number three: T was somewhere behind me, yelling.

"Come back here, you bastard! I ain't finished with you yet!"

For someone who was now totally insane, I was able to piece the situation together pretty quickly: I had passed out for a moment, but not before my stubbornly swelling cock had helped to pry me out of range of T and his tickling tool. I was free, thanks to my dick! "Good boy," I whispered to my aching pet. I stretched my arms and managed to move another millimeter forward as T screamed and ranted behind me.

There was no reason to believe I would end up anywhere but in some dark pit full of rubble. But insanity was now the norm, and if it was insane to keep trying, then that was good enough to keep my hips and fingertips working, even my tortured toes joining in the effort. Soon T gave up screaming at me, and I had the sound of my own breath to keep me company—breath that rattled and grunted like a worn-out engine pulling me along, dragging my hard-on with me. If I could make any sense out of the darkness, it looked as if I might not have far to go. Just a couple more feet and I would be at the edge. Of something.

When I was close enough, I stretched my tired arms to reach and grab onto the edge of the vent opening I now faced. Finally, an end to my sweaty metal prison! But the edge was sharp, so I moved carefully, encouraged only by what seemed to be, if not a light in the distance, a lesser degree of darkness. Hitching myself forward slowly, I was able at last to let my arms dangle beneath me into the half-light. But I had no time to even raise my head and look around before my arms were grabbed and nearly pulled from their sockets.

"Got you now, prick!"

Somehow T had figured out where I would emerge and had found a way to get to it. I scarcely had time to register my surprise, I was begging him to go easy as he pulled me out of the duct: "Hey hey hey watch my dick, watch my dick, watch my dick!"

"I'll do more than watch your dick, asshole. I'll do a *hell* of a lot more!"

With a *whump* I landed on the floor, which as far as I could see was a white tiled floor like the one I'd left behind, in what seemed like a former lifetime. T stood over me, his coverall unzipped. If my own stupid prick was still engorged, his was positively rapturous, a gravity-defying ramrod swinging wildly in a victory dance. He asked in a husky voice, "Are you ready for what's coming to you?"

"Oh, absolutely!" I slid to the middle of the corridor, the better to spread myself out, my arms above my head. "Go ahead, you bastard," I said, writhing, offering up my bare feet. "Tickle me to death! Go ahead!"

"You're grinning now," he said, unsuccessfully stifling his own grin. "You have no idea what agony this is going to be!"

I added a laugh to my grin. "Ha! Do your worst, you big dumb piece of meat!"

He stood over me, reaching down. It took all of my will to keep my eyes open. It's a good thing I did, or I wouldn't have seen what happened next, it came so quickly: hands appeared, several of them, grabbing T and pulling him from view. There was a sound of scuffling, some urgent, heavy breathing, then nothing.

III. MY NAME IS ALDEBARAN

1. THE NAMES OF STARS

I was always the kind of guy you could count on, and always had something with me that I could count on—a notebook, a cassette recorder, a watch. I kept pace with the clock and the calendar, second-guessing each minute, forecasting the end of each day before breakfast was over. So I had to learn the hard way—the hardest way imaginable—to adapt to a life where I couldn't plan beyond my next step. Because the step after that could be a plunge into the unknown, so deep I might never come back.

There were seven of us. We kept mostly to our "safe area," a small auditorium or lecture hall where the seats had been removed, only empty risers facing the dusty podium below. That first night I slept on the top riser, just because I wanted to be near a wall. Exhausted, I passed out the moment I hit the floor. Then I woke suddenly in the pitch dark, not knowing where I was or what had roused me.

"M? Is that you?"

It was the villain formerly known as T-49, who had chased me into this unlikely space. A chill went through me, unconnected to the fact that I was stretched out naked on the floor: not long ago this same man had been chasing me down hallways, threatening my life. But instead of trying to scuttle away in the darkness, or calling for help, I said only, "That's not my name anymore."

A wet, heavy sigh sounded somewhere to my left. "What's your name?"

"Aldebaran."

"Jesus Christ."

"You've got a new name, too."

"Yeah...." The unmistakable sound of beefy flesh settling down on wood. He was on the floor now, maybe an arm's length away. "I want to stretch out next to you. You okay with that?"

I started trembling. I couldn't help it, the events of earlier that day were fresh in my mind. But everything was different now. So I ended up saying, "Sure," and moved closer to the wall so he could snuggle up to me, as if we did this all the time.

***

When I had emerged from that aluminum duct—the same duct that other men had used, unknowingly, to find this place—to lie writhing on the floor, insanely begging T to tickle me to death, only to witness his miraculous abduction by hands reaching out from nowhere to pull him into the darkness, I was no more eager to move forward than to try and crawl back to the hell I'd escaped from. Added to that was the dizzying feeling of not knowing if any of this was real.

Was I hallucinating? Was I dead?

In the end it was raging thirst that got me moving again. Weak and shaky, I struggled to my feet and stumbled forward, toward the spot where T had stood a few minutes before. If I could only hear a sound, even T's voice threatening me again, it would be better than the silence surrounding me.

It didn't last, though. Moving those few inches were all it took to make things happen. From either side hands appeared—I felt rather than saw them—and gripped my arms. Weak and dazed, scared and curious, I let myself be pulled into the darkness. Soon I was in a dimly lit stairwell, two shaggy men in the famous gray coveralls half-pulling, half-carrying me down to the floor below. Those coveralls were in even worse shape than mine, filthy and in shreds. This scene was a setup for more terror, more despair; and yet, having been manhandled and abused for so long, I could recognize something different happening here. Beneath their urgency there was something respectful, almost tender in the way these men were gripping me, as though I were an accident victim being rushed toward some life-saving procedure.

That didn't mean I wasn't angry. *I will never be touched again* was what ran through my mind, over and over. *No matter what, I will never be touched.* Only my unworkable tongue, thick with thirst, kept me from saying it out loud.

The end of the journey lay beyond a door that creaked so loudly it shocked my ears, which had heard nothing but scuffling and breathing for some time—that, and the deep rumbling voice of one of the men carrying me. *It's okay, you'll be okay,* he kept saying. After one turn, then another, we were in a room of uncertain dimensions and levels, dark except for candles flickering in the stale air. Naked men moved through a funk of sweat and semen, casting dim elongated shadows. It was as if I'd been carried through time as well as space, back to a prehistoric era. I nearly jumped when the deep calm voice returned, asking a question this time: "Are you all right?"

Still shaking, not totally convinced I wasn't dead, I tried to speak, to say how thirsty I was. I took a breath, held it, and set it free, but no words came with it. A hand stroked my arm, and from another direction came a cup of water. It wasn't cold or fresh, but I swallowed it in two gulps and handed it back for more. Who were these men? Was my presence here a good thing? Was I...could I even imagine it...*free*? That thought didn't last long, as I heard, from not far away, an outraged sputtering that soon dissolved into laughter. It was T's voice, and when I understood what was happening to him I nearly fainted. Sure enough, this place was just another venue for more of the same treatment—possibly worse, since these men looked even less civilized than my former captors did. Despite my weakness my resolve was stronger than ever: *Don't fucking touch me.*

"Don't worry," the voice said. "It's not what you think. That guy who was threatening you, he was in a rage. We're tickling him to calm him down."

Another cup of water and I still hadn't found my voice: *Don't fucking touch....*

"Come here and see."

We moved in darkness through another doorway, its perfect rectangle and the cool tile under my feet the only signs that we weren't actually in a cave. There was candlelight here too, and it showed T spread-eagle on the floor, pinned down by two men as two others tickled his neck and ears with some kind of feathery white cloth. T was giggling so rapidly he could hardly draw breath. We had to keep well back from his wildly kicking legs, even as the kicking began to subside along with the desperate thrusting of his hips.

"You see," my escort said, "they're not really torturing him, just tickling him till he's helpless, so he can't do any harm."

As T calmed down, nothing moving but his chest struggling for air, the two men who were holding him down turned their attention to his midsection, freeing his thick cock from his coverall, stroking the shaft, tickling his balls so that he was both laughing and moaning, sinking into an eroticized state.

When my voice finally came, it did not bring my internal *I-will-not-be-touched* mantra with it. To my surprise I asked a question instead: "What is that white stuff?"

"Gauze. We're in a hospital, the subbasement of an old dead hospital." The deep voice was so close now that I could feel warm breath coming with it. "See, we're escapees, just like you. And someday, maybe very soon, we're going to get the fuck out of here."

His words, like the erotic spectacle I was witnessing, eased the tension that had been so much a part of my days I could hardly stand up without it. I let myself sink to the floor. In my state of exhaustion it was a luxury just to rest my back against the wall and watch the two naked ticklers who were attending so lovingly to T's cock and balls. From what I could see by candlelight, one of these men was a tall, muscular blond, just about T's equal in size; the other had a smaller, wiry build. I turned my head to get a better look at the man who had been speaking to me. He was naked too, and even in the candlelight the curly tufts of hair covering him all over were resplendent, his long, thick cock erect as he continued to stand next to me and watch.

T's cries were now those of a man who needed to come. While one of the men pumped his dick expertly with one hand and tickled his balls with the other, his partner moved down to T's feet. Somewhere along the way his boots and socks had been removed, his long, strong-looking feet now vulnerable to the fingers that began stroking them, caressing first the tops of the feet, then the soles. As the fingers moved faster, dancing along the ticklish skin, T's cries rose in pitch. I marveled at how fast the jacking fist moved, how deftly those fingers covered every inch of T's feet. The jackhammer thrusting of his pelvis grew wilder, and instinctively I pulled my stretched-out legs back as he came, his cum hitting the tile audibly, like huge raindrops. Even the wall beside me was wet and glistening. The two men who had brought T to his release now stood up and stroked their own dicks till they shot over T's chest and belly.

The man standing beside me was moaning, pumping his own dick, which was almost close enough for me to take in my mouth. But there was *no way*. And there was no way that any of these men were going to touch *me*.

Again it was as if he had read my mind. Sinking to the floor, he turned and felt my hard dick through my coverall. As he reached for the zipper-pull at my neck I grabbed his wrist. It was time to say the words that had been running through my mind all this time. But when I tried to speak my voice was hard to modulate, like a teenage boy's; and what I'd intended to be bold came out wistful instead. "If I were smart," I said, "I'd never let a man touch me again."

His answer was quick: "Nobody's that smart." He lowered his mouth toward mine.

"Wait," I said, "*tell* me. What is this place? How many of us are there? Are we going to get out? *When*?"

"Sorry," he said. He laid a hand on my thigh, but the touch was reassuring. "Like I said before, it looks like this used to be a hospital. Apparently the Compound converted part of it to their use. The rest of it just sits here, falling apart."

"How big is it?"

"We haven't gone far. It's dangerous. There's at least one more level under this one, and there are too many gaps in the floor. Mostly we stay in this area. There's not much else to see. Smaller rooms. Some old equipment, nothing much of use. And not an envelope or scrap of letterhead to tell us exactly where we are."

The tone of his voice was calm, as before; but the more he talked, the less safe I felt. "They know we're here," I said.

"Some of them know," he said. "The ones who are helping us. The women."

"What women?"

"Please let me touch you."

I resisted the impulse to slap his hand. "Horny bastard."

He lowered his hand, stroked his dick a few times, then ran his fingers through his head of thick curly hair. "Try to understand," he said. "We might be caught and killed any minute. This crumbling building might fall on us. We're dirty as shit and we don't get enough water to drink or food to eat." This time his hand found my zipper-pull; he lowered it enough to press his face against my hairy chest. "Living this close to the edge makes you want to...."

His mention of food made *me* want to eat. Very suddenly my hunger was as wild as the thirst I'd felt earlier. I looked up, and as if there were such a thing as instant gratification, there was another man kneeling down next to me with a bowl of food. Crusts of bread, some kind of processed meat—I held the bowl and chewed like a dog, shamelessly licking the bottom and sides when the meat was gone. "Is there more?"

"Not right now. Take this." It was half a cupful of tepid water, and I gulped it down too. This man held a match to a candle stub near his other side, and I got a better look at him, how beautiful his skin was in the glow, dusky and gleaming. Now he raised the candle flame between our faces and I looked into the eyes of... Duke. If it weren't for the candle flame between us, I would have thrown my arms around him, crushed the breath out of him in sheer joy. Instead I raised my hand and stroked the side of his face.

His eyes were shining. He took my hand, squeezed my fingers. "Never thought I'd see you again."

"Duke...."

He laughed. "Nobody's called me that in a while," he said.

"For a long time I was L-22. Now they call me Beetlejuice. 'B' for short."

"Betelgeuse," my rescuer said to B and me. Having unburied his face from my chest while I was eating, he was stroking me now, from my shoulder to my waist. "The twelfth brightest star in the sky. Also known as Orion's armpit."

"Thanks a lot, Dogface," said B.

"I don't get it," I said. There was too much, way too much in this new scene to take in, and the sudden ingestion of food was making me sleepy, in spite of my rock-hard dick.

"We've all taken the names of stars, courtesy of my astronomy background. Some of us can't remember our real names, anyway. I'm Sirius."

"You'd damn well better be serious."

"No." He laughed, raising his eyes toward mine. His eyeglasses had been taped together in half a dozen places. "Sirius, as in the dog star. Because I'm so hairy."

"Not a very flattering name."

"It's a good name. Next to the sun, Sirius is the brightest star in the sky."

I let myself relax a bit more into the wall. It seemed like the first time in years that I was relaxed at all. But speaking of names...I was M-36, the last time I thought about it, but before that....

I looked up at B and asked, "What's my real name? Can you tell me?"

"Rand," he said, stroking my hair. "Your name is Rand."

Of course. Always Rand, never Randy, which I hated. Still it seemed strange, a name I couldn't fit my own lips to.

"But I'm going to call you Aldebaran," Sirius said. "That's one of my favorites."

"You're crazy." A sound bubbled up in my throat and came

out as a laugh—not the tortured kind that had all but replaced my speech, but the amused kind.

"He sure is." B sank down on the other side of me. "We're all fucking crazy. That's the whole point."

From the direction where T-49 had been pinned to the floor came a series of sharp grunts. He was coming again.

"We do a lot of that around here," Sirius said.

"I can tell," I said. "The air reeks of it. Cum, and candle wax, and—something else."

"That would be the slop bucket." T-49's prolonged orgasm ended in a great sigh. Sirius turned his head toward the sound. "I think I'm going to call your well-built friend Pollux. It's a star, and also another name for Hercules."

"It might be premature to call him my friend," I said. "When you found us he was trying to kill me."

"Don't worry, he won't hurt you. A few more orgasms like that and he'll be as gentle as a kitten."

Exhausted as I was, I didn't know if I would ever have an orgasm again. But with Sirius stretched out on my right side and B on my left, both men stroking and playing with my skin, exposing more and more of it, my hard dick got even harder.

"You can get out of your coverall," Sirius said. "We usually only wear them on supply runs."

Supply runs? There was still so much I had to learn about this new setting. For now I let myself drift like a gently rocking boat, the stroking of the men like waves lapping at my sides. They managed, very tenderly, to relieve me of my coverall, boots, and socks. Fingers teased my cock, slid along my scrotum, and there was no name for what they were doing there but *tickling*. "Oh, Jesus, that feels good," I heard myself saying. Then I heard Sirius: "I want your cock in my mouth." It was his wetness, then, settling firmly around my shaft, and B's mouth on mine, his tongue pouring into me, warm and shivering. I hadn't been kissed like that for a long time and didn't want it to end, the tip of his tongue tickling my palate as an unvoiced moan rose within me, a soft vibration at the back of my throat. I relaxed more deeply, thrusting my hips toward Sirius as B tongued my mouth and also began massaging my ribs. When hands touched my feet I wasn't even startled; I let them be stroked lovingly, tantalizingly, as a tear rolled down my cheek, spilling from a well of feeling that had nothing to do with grief and stress and everything to do with fulfillment.

Later, when my mouth was free, I whispered, "This is better than the fucking Chamber."

2. RIGEL WENT DOWN

Sirius and Arcturus took the lead. Behind them, Betelgeuse held my hand. And behind us, Vega and Pollux walked together like a short-and-tall comedy team. Polaris, the young soldier, took up the rear. In addition to the usual ration of food and water, we were hoping to get more on this supply run: candles, matches, flashlight batteries, a small cache of first aid supplies, maybe a fresh blanket or two. Anything else we would get depended on what the women were able to bring. We were careful not to ask for too much—they were risking their own lives, after all.

Sirius, in addition to being the unofficial leader of the group, was also the keeper of time, which he kept stashed in a pocket of his coverall—a woman's wristwatch with no band and a nearly inscrutable face smaller than a dime. It could only be read by flashlight, another precious resource that couldn't be squandered. So it was up to Sirius to tell us when it was day or night, when to bed down, when it was time for a supply run. The watch proved that what he had told me was true—it was the women of the Compound, led by Crystal, who were helping us. They had known their own form of oppression, so much so that they had begun to see our freedom as their own, and had formed a secret network to try to bring it about.

I recalled walking with Crystal, back when I was M-36, observing her thoughtfulness and assuming that her thoughts were far away from me and the others who shared my fate. It never occurred to me to ask her for help. It seemed to be enough that she did not personally wish me harm. Now I was asked to believe that she and the other women risked their lives to bring us food and water and plan our escape. It was unbelievable. But I remembered the day, during my period as a trusty, when I saw one of the men casually backhand his wife across the face. She didn't cry out, or react in any way except to cast her eyes downward—which spoke volumes about the act, about the way these men felt toward their women, and how the women had been trained to respond. If I had been able to look more closely I might have found some shadow of resentment in the somber look I had so often seen on Crystal's face.

"And exactly how," I asked Sirius, "are we supposed to escape? A bunch of naked, filthy men who look like they've been living in a cave for months?"

"Don't worry," he said, "they've got a plan." He placed a flashlight in my hand. "Right now it's time for a supply run. That'll get your adrenaline pumping again."

So there we were, in a wide corridor as treacherous now as it must once have been safe. With gaps in the floor and broken masonry hanging overhead, it was a hundred feet of hell, especially since the floor was not through crumbling, and as you took a cautious step with your right foot the tile might give way under your left. What had once been solid was now buckled and warped, curled, and curdled, rows of tile poking up like teeth or dropping out of sight. The prize for losing this crapshoot was to plunge into darkness and never be seen again. That, as I was reminded often, was what had happened to Rigel. A sudden crack, a shout, and he was gone.

"How far down does it go?" I whispered to Sirius. We were all whispering, as if our normal voices would summon more crumbling doom.

"Take a look."

Very carefully I got as close as I could to the edge of the nearest hole. The beam of my flashlight, swallowed up by darkness and dust, showed nothing.

"There's some kind of subbasement down there. When Rigel went down, he was killed immediately. That's what we hope, anyway. If he screamed again, we never heard him."

"You didn't try to go down there?"

"Nope. The stairwell ends at a door that's been sealed, and trying to lower ourselves through any of these holes in the floor would be too risky."

"All this damn chattering is making me nervous." That was Arcturus, who usually didn't admit to nervousness. In spite of the weakened condition that we all shared, he could lift and carry more than any of us, even Pollux. Built like a bear, with a deep growling voice to match, he looked as if he could crush you to death like a grizzly.

"Sorry," I said. "Sirius was just showing me...."

"If you want to see something, look over there." Arcturus pointed his light at the wall to our left and about a dozen feet ahead. "That's where Rigel went down, on that exact spot." There was a hole in the floor, right next to the wall—a hole large enough for a man to fall through. "He thought the floor would be more solid next to the wall. Didn't take more than two steps before he fell."

"Oh, shit." That was B, on my left, his free hand tightening its grip on mine. "Don't remind me, man. I nearly fell myself, trying to get over there to see what happened. I shine my light down there, and there's *nothin'* to see. He was gone, just like that."

"His theory was sound, though." That was Polaris, an ex-soldier. As shaggy-headed and bearded as any of us, there was still something about him of the crewcut, smooth-shaven recruit. He had the erect posture and precise walk of a drill sergeant, and his entire life might have been different if his ROTC buddies hadn't found out, at a crucial moment in his life, how ticklish he was. That had led him down the erotic path that had in turn led him here. "The floor *should* be more solid next to the wall."

"*Should be* don't count for shit," Arcturus said. At last he turned his light away from the spot where Rigel went down. It amazed me that he had the guts to look at all, for Rigel and Arcturus had been lovers, as close as two men could be. These days Arcturus kept to himself, not saying much, never joining us in our erotic diversions.

"Let's keep to the way we've been going," Sirius said. "And just be fucking *careful*."

We moved in a slow, shuffling silence, until Vega piped up again. Complaining about the women now. "Is this really the *best* they could do? Couldn't they have found a better way to get supplies to us?"

"Shut the fuck up," Sirius said. "This whole deal had to be *improvised*, okay? We're still safe back in our safe area, that's the main thing."

"Safe till they find us, you mean."

"Fucking Vega," Pollux mumbled. "Too scared to come with us, too scared to be left behind."

"I know the best way to deal with Vega," Arcturus said. It was true. Back in our safe area Vega moved like a cat, refusing to be cornered, not even by a tireless pursuer like Pollux. But more than once Arcturus, infuriated by Vega's mouthiness, had managed to catch the smaller man and nearly tickle him to death. There were scars on his torso from cigarette burns, remains of an abused childhood that had left him high-strung, pessimistic, and desperate for affection. More so than any of us, he couldn't stand to be tickled for long, but he was always horny and it didn't take long to get him hard and bring him off. Once he'd shot his load, he'd be up and running again, crying *We'll never get out of here* or, even worse, *They know we're here, you know they do, they'll pick us off one by one!*

When I woke up each day the question was always, not *whether* I would have someone's dick in my mouth within a few minutes, but *whose* dick would it be. Vega's was often first. He was always ready, like the pup who has to be first at the food bowl. Then there was Pollux, who was a footfucker from way back but who could also be a brutal mouthfucker, pounding my warm wet cave like a force of nature—a hammering ocean or blinding rain that could only be endured. Sirius was slick and sweet; I could wrap my tongue around him and slurp him down like an ice-cream soda. More than any of us he took solace in sex, comfort in as much contact as possible. Given to flights of wild imagining, sometimes he made the most sense when he was being sucked off, his cock pumping out neurotic energy, leaving his mind clearer. Polaris was quick, for he liked to jack himself off till he was on the brink of shooting, then force his dickhead between my lips already spurting, filling my cheeks with his heavy load.

But my favorite was B. His cock slid into my mouth in a way that completed me, its rigid heat filling a space custom-made to take it in, his dickhead firm and luscious as a plum against my palate. His thrusts and moans, the shuddering of his thighs, his rocking and swaying as if he might pass out from pleasure…it was fine. And unlike Vega or Polaris, who hopped off like bees seeking the next pollen-pot, B would always return the favor, aligning himself so he could suck me off without dislodging his own still-sweet dick from my mouth.

Like Arcturus, the three men known as The Lost Ones did not circulate through our endless roundelay. Poor souls who had completely cracked under the torture administered by the Compound, these wild-eyed droolers kept to themselves, in a hallway off the side of the auditorium, playing endless tickling games on each other's skin. Sometimes their groans and shrieks were almost unbearable. We made sure they got enough food and water to survive, but it was best, we knew, to stay away from them.

"Watch it!"

I swung my flashlight beam alongside B's, following the sound of cascading rubble. Another section of floor had fallen, far enough away to be of no immediate danger—and yet, what could have made it fall but the vibration of our boots? And how much longer before the whole bloody place caved in? We kept moving forward, but slowly, very slowly. Dust gathered like fog in our flashlight beams, creaks and rustlings swarmed around our ears. Never had a structure seemed more alive, more threatening. I could barely control my breathing, and the hairs on the back of my neck wouldn't stay down. I knew that the women would be coming down to the floor above, that they'd deliver the supplies through a trap door in the ceiling that lay at the end of this treacherous path. I didn't want to think, though, of making the return trip with my arms full of heavy supplies, and how much more treacherous that would be.

When we finally reached the end of the corridor, Sirius climbed up the improvised stepladder of bricks and boards and knocked on the ceiling. The seven of us held our collective breath, waiting, Sirius burning precious flashlight batteries keeping his beam aimed upward. When the trap door opened and a face appeared, suddenly glowing in the light, it looked like a projected image of Crystal, a ghost version of the face I used to see each morning and night. Yes, I had seen her get hit once, too, and never remembered it till now. She had brought water to some of the men who were working up a thirst in the village square, tickling a victim who had just been brought in that day. The brute who took the first cupful of water sipped once, then threw the rest of the cupful back in her face. *Not cold enough*, he said. That was back before I was a trusty, and I was only semiconscious, being dragged from one torture to the next; how could I be so sure now that that was what I saw? But her glowing face brought back another image, another memory: she had cut my hair. In the cell where I'd slept as a trusty, she had put a towel around my shoulders and cut my hair, trimmed my beard. How many times had that happened? Christ, how long had it been? I wanted to call out to her now, but it wasn't the time or place. There would never be a time or place.

At least two more women were there—I saw that many more hands—and they helped pass down the supplies to Sirius, who in turn handed them from his shaky perch to our waiting arms. It all went without a word, as if the anxious women and trembling men were in two separate dimensions that couldn't communicate. Then I heard Crystal speaking, in the calm tones I remembered so well: "We've got one more thing. Be careful, it's very warm. You'll have to hand it back up to me when you're through. Hurry."

It was an aluminum tub with a lid; Arcturus stepped up to help Sirius lower it from the ceiling. When he pried up the lid, steam rose around its edges. Having not seen anything warmer than a candle flame for so long, we were like primitives witnessing fire for the first time. But what we had was more wonderful than fire: hot towels, two stacks of them, moist and steaming. With trembling hands we grabbed them, rubbed our hands and faces.

Then, seeing Crystal had temporarily withdrawn, we unzipped our coveralls, let them fall around our ankles, and rubbed ourselves down. It was impossible not to moan with pleasure. We wiped ourselves, and we wiped each other down—chests and armpits, itchy asses. I took a fresh towel and lovingly bathed B's dick and scrotum.

By the time Crystal reappeared—it couldn't have been more than a couple of minutes—we had zipped up our coveralls and tossed the towels back in the tub. They were fit for nothing but disposal, but the tub needed to be put back where it belonged. Sirius handed it up to her waiting arms. She took it away, then returned.

"One more thing," she said, and motioned for Sirius to try to get closer to the ceiling. He climbed farther up the makeshift stool of bricks and boards, and a great deal of fast whispering took place. A tingling ran up my spine—not an unusual event, given the nature of this place, except this was a kind of panic I had not felt in a while. The way Sirius stood there, whispering in the dark for what seemed like forever, talking with his hands in his nervousness, made me want to get moving again, quickly, back to our safe area. Vega didn't help, he was at my elbow chattering softly: "What are they saying, what are they talking about, what's taking so long? What *is* there to talk about, except escaping?"

"Sshhh," I said.

When Sirius turned toward us again I couldn't resist shining my flashlight in his face, seeking some clue about what was just discussed. Along with the annoyance of having my light turned on him like that, his face displayed some perplexity, as if he'd just been told something that was hard to believe.

"Arcturus, come help me. The rest of you move back a little, we'll need some room."

We waited, somewhat uneasily, to see what else might be coming through that small square opening. Vega still danced at my elbow, and I wanted to backhand him into another time zone, but I also wanted to keep my eyes on the ceiling. To my surprise it looked, at first, as if a load of potatoes was coming through—a length of burlap, a sack. As it grew in size it reminded me more of the sack that Michael had brought me here in. By the time it was lowered down into the waiting arms of the two men, it was clear that its contents had the shape of a body—one that wasn't moving much, except as gravity dictated. Very carefully Sirius and Arcturus laid the sack on the corridor floor.

Pollux spoke for all of us: "So who the hell is it? And what are we supposed to do with him?"

"To answer your second question first," Sirius said, "we can do whatever we want with him. But get ready for a shock when you see who it is."

Arcturus helped undo the cords that were binding the top of the sack, and together he and Sirius pulled the burlap down until a red sweaty face appeared. I had never seen that face before, those eyes rolling in panic, mouth obscured by duct tape—and yet I *had*. It was a matter of context, of needing to see the oppressor as a captive. I blinked, and blinked again, and the features arranged themselves into the face of Michael Loomis. "Jesus Christ," I said, taking an involuntary step back, bumping into B, who had stepped forward for a look. "Holy shit," he breathed in my ear. The others came forward, carefully, one by one, each following his shock with a soft curse, an offering to the unguessable nature of fate. Not all of us had known Granger, there being more than one "recruiter" for this place; but we had all known Michael— known him as well, it seemed, as we had ever known anyone, his body, his smell, his *mind* imposed on each of us, clinging to us like barnacle on rock. We had all spent days in his bleak farmhouse, hearing his story when it wasn't drowned out by our own screams; we had all made the journey in a burlap bag on the floor of his blue panel truck, to be unceremoniously dumped on the front lawn of the Compound. That was part of our wonder as we stood there: that this madman who had so indelibly worked his will on each of us should appear now, as if our collective memory had summoned him from the darkness and dust of our subbasement prison.

Pollux turned his head and spat in the dust. "What the hell are we supposed to do, drag him all the way back to our safe place?"

"Who knows, it might be worth it," Arcturus said, licking his lips. He ran the toe of his boot along the length of the sack, poking it here and there. "Might well be worth it." He seemed to be trying to make eye contact with Michael, whose eyes kept darting from one of us to another.

Vega clawed his way forward for a better look. "Oh, I want him," he said, his voice trembling. "I want him so bad."

"But *why him?*" Pollux asked, shaking his head as if to clear away this vision.

"It's a sign," Sirius said. His voice trembled too, not with lust or anger but with something more rare: hope. "It means the women's revolt has started. It means we might get out of here soon."

A mixture of anxiety and excitement stirred all of us. We moved restlessly, shaking our heads in disbelief, cursing to ourselves. Stealing glances at the face of the man in the sack, the face that stayed there no matter how often we looked, refusing to vanish like a dream.

It was Polaris who spoke up next. "I say we dump him. Dump him down a hole right now. We don't need him, and it's too dangerous, trying to drag him back."

But dumping him seemed even more unthinkable than trying to bring him back with us, if only because...*Michael Loomis*. The reality of him struck me again, and something began crawling up my spine—the mute, sightless part of myself that had been waiting patiently, in the dark, for revenge. *Michael Loomis*. My palms began to itch, and my dick stirred.

"I wish Rigel was here," B said. "He'd know what to do."

"What did Crystal say?" Polaris asked. "What was their intention in turning him over to us?"

"You've gotta ask?" Vega said. "We don't need to be told. They want him to get a taste of his own medicine, that's what!"

Sirius wiped his mouth with the back of his hand. "God help me," he said, "but I want to give it to him."

The way back should have been easier, but our steps were not retraceable. It was as if the gaps in the floor had shifted since we'd threaded our way through the first time. And our progress was slow, agonizingly slow now that we were loaded down with supplies and dragging an extra burden too. I ended up with two sacks of food and two jugs of water, clutching a sack in each fist and a jug handle on each thumb. The pull on my arms made me doubt I'd last five steps; but if everyone else was going to make a good show of it—even Vega was carrying two sacks almost bigger than himself—then I was damned if I wouldn't as well. I carried my flashlight in my armpit, its beam sometimes swinging off in useless directions. Only Sirius and Arcturus each had one hand free so they could keep their flashlights steadily aimed at the path they were taking, and it was up to the rest of us to follow their movements carefully. Before long we were sweating torrents, the scrappy coveralls plastered to our skins, the feel of the hot cleansing towels just a distant memory. We were panting too, with effort and anxiety. "Jesus *Christ* this is dangerous," Vega said at one point, and for once nobody told him to shut up. But B and Pollux had the most dangerous job, dragging the sack with Michael Loomis in it. His muscular bulk was made to cave in a fragile floor, and I expected to hear it give way any second.

"B," Pollux said, "don't wrap the cord around your wrist like that. If he goes down, you don't want to go too."

"It was a hell of a lot easier," B said, "for him to haul me than the other way around."

"Just wait," Vega muttered. "Just wait till we get him out of that sack."

By the time we finally made it to the auditorium my arms were aching and my feet were sore. My work as a trusty had prepared me for lifting and carrying, but the subsistence diet I now followed had turned my muscles to mush. I didn't say anything, was determined not to limp as we stored the food and water in a small room at the rear of the auditorium. Candles, matches, batteries, blankets, and the first aid kit were stashed there too. The door didn't lock, but as a depository it was better than nothing. We learned to keep an eye on it so the Lost Ones wouldn't get into the supplies. They were out now, gibbering at us as we stowed away the goods, so what with our grunting and groaning and cursing with relief that we had made it back safe, the room was noisier than usual. Flashlight beams played carelessly across the walls, as if we wouldn't be running dangerously low on batteries again within a few days. I sat down with my back against a wall, looking over the chaotic scene. I knew what everyone was thinking about, because I was, too: it was time to turn our attention to Michael Loomis.

Between the two of them, Pollux and Polaris got our new guest out of the sack. He lay on the floor, naked, his mouth taped shut, bound at the wrists and ankles. How humiliating it must have been, to be captured by women and stripped naked, bound and gagged. And frightening as hell, not knowing what they were going to do with him. Now he lay trembling before us, probably bleeding internally from sheer panic, but trying not to show it. His semi-engorged dick lay up on his belly; how well I understood that, the hard-on of fear.

"Let's get a better look at him," Pollux said, grabbing his bound wrists and raising them over his head, lifting him to his feet. He was at least a head shorter than Pollux but powerfully built, and he was hairy—not hairy like Sirius, who was curly from his shoulders to his toes, but hairy with a fine red fuzz that clung teasingly to his pecs, peeked out mischievously from his armpits. In the candlelight his semi-hard, circumcised dick had a red, delicately chafed look that made me want to take it in my mouth. Oh yes, Michael made urges bubble beneath my skin, gave me lucid dreams where I did the impossible, taking his dick in my mouth *and* shoving my tongue up his ass at the same time.

But mainly, of course, I wanted to tickle him. I wanted to feel his helplessness, hear him howl the way I'd howled under his hands. I wanted him to *know* something of what he had put me through.

I looked around. The stirring of cocks and backhanded wiping of wet mouths proved well enough that we were on the same wavelength. It was just a matter of converging to devour the meat. And yet, from somewhere in my head came a warning, a softer-than-a-whisper instruction to *not do this*.

"Wait," I said.

The looks I got: wait for fucking *what*? Pollux, with a superhuman effort, lifted our prize by the forearms and looped the cord between his wrists over a fluorescent light fixture

[163]

hanging from the ceiling. Then he moved up a table, shoved it right under our prisoner so that he sat now with his legs straight in front of him, the tender soles of his feet, bound together at the ankles, facing us.

"Good, but not good enough," Sirius said. "We have to bind his feet separately, to the corners of the table. That way we can do them real good, and get at his thighs better, too."

Pollux untied Michael's ankles, grasped one and pulled it toward the corner of the table. "Cords, please," he said.

"Wait," I said, "wait wait wait."

"What is it *now?*" Polaris asked. I had thought of him as a man of reason, so proud of his disciplined military background, but now he was just a pair of fired-up eyes telling me to get out of the way.

"This is wrong," I said.

With his free foot Michael kicked, whirred his leg through the air like a blade. That didn't stop B from approaching him. "That's right, my man. Just kick the shit out of the air. Use up all the energy you got."

"Wait," I said again. "Wait a minute. Let's think about this."

"Always the thinker," Sirius said. Curling his upper lip. Where was *this* coming from? If anyone had respect for thinking, it was him.

"You're scaring me," I told him.

"Fuck being scared. Don't you see what this is? This guy's touched every one of his with his stinking hands, with his ropes and cords and feathers and brushes. He kept on touching us when we begged him with our last breath to stop. He laughed in our faces while he drove us over the edge again and again." He took a step forward. His legs were shaking. "And as if that wasn't enough, he brought us to this place."

His speech moved the others. They stepped forward, a horizontal forest of hard-ons.

"Wait, wait," I said. "This is wrong. It means we're no better than he is."

"And does anybody," Arcturus growled, "give a flying fuck about that?"

***

This is wrong—that phrase and I had a history, stretching back to the last afternoon that Kyle and I spent together.

We'd been smoking dope on that hot Saturday, then driving around in Kyle's van. I watched Kyle at the wheel, inscrutable in his sunglasses, his head half-turned as if he could watch me and the road at the same time. I was watching him, always, wondering what he was thinking. I was in love with him, and surprised that love could be so punishing, a constant craving to know the unknowable. What was Kyle thinking? Was he thinking of me? Why or why not? We were so close, as close as two people could be; yet I didn't know him at all. Here we were, swinging down the narrow road near one of the busier beaches, and he was describing this fantasy he had while I half-dozed, my head bobbing like a senseless thing against the headrest. *Was it a fantasy, or was it something that really happened, or could happen?* It was a kidnapping he was talking about, a kidnapping on a road like this, late on a Saturday afternoon. Some younger kid—Tommy Hatch, say—could be standing by the side of the road, hitching a ride home. We could stop, offer him a ride, then take him back to Kyle's room, and tie him up.

I knew Tommy Hatch. He was fourteen, two years younger than me, but taller, on the skinny side. He tended to go barefoot and shirtless as much as possible. Even when we were little kids in grade school, he was always taking his shoes and socks off at recess and running barefoot across the playground. On a hot day he was the first to roll his t-shirt up and walk around with his flat brown belly exposed. He also stood out because he didn't wear boxer-type swim trunks but the kind that looked more like Jockey shorts, only a lot smaller. He was the kind of kid who always wore a snotty look, too, his eyes half-closed, the corners of his mouth turned down. That image of Tommy, the look on his face and the way his sandy hair fell across his forehead, took all my attention, reducing Kyle's speech to a background hum; and I realized something that had never entered my conscious thoughts before—Tommy was *sexy*. That soporific look on his face was really saying, *I'm so heavy with urges between my sweaty legs that I can barely keep my eyes open.* All summer I'd been thinking of nothing and no one but Kyle, and how strange it was now to fasten on the idea that other boys could be sexy too. Sexy, and maybe even willing.

I was still picturing Tommy in his red trunks, that big bulge between his legs, when the van slowed down and I opened my eyes to see him at the side of the road with those same trunks on and nothing else, just a towel across his shoulders, his thumb stuck out to hitch a ride. To suddenly see him like that was so startling that I broke out in a kind of paranoid sweat, and wondered if the pot we'd smoked had had something else in it that was making me hallucinate. Kyle slowed down, began to turn the wheel, and I reached out to touch his knee and said, "Careful," as if he might be under the same spell, and that image of Tommy was really a pine tree just waiting for a van to come along and crash into it. I still didn't believe it was Tommy—at best I thought maybe it was a cardboard cutout of him propped up by the side of the road—

till Kyle leaned across me and called out the window, "Hey, you can ride with us, but you'll have to get in the back," and Tommy shrugged, fluttering his half-closed eyelids and sweeping his sandy hair out of his eyes.

This is it, I thought, not even knowing what "it" was, cracking open my door so I could climb down and open the rear door of the van for Tommy. Before I slid from my seat Kyle grabbed my wrist.

"You know what to do," he said.

Did I? True, the erotic cellar of my mind was bursting with ideas, but they were all half-formed, faceless. I felt a distinct sense of unreality as I led Tommy to the back of the van and opened the door. As he was climbing in, his red trunks nearly revealing the crack of his ass, I touched his lower back, as if to help him up but really just because I wanted to. His skin, so slick and hot and firm, was filled with possibilities. I was shaking as I climbed in behind him and closed the door. Kyle took off, none too gently, and Tommy and I rocked around on our knees, trying to get our balance. This was my chance to get next to him without making him suspect anything. "Oops," I said, intentionally falling right on top of him. In the closeness of the van he smelled of cocoa butter and sweat. I reached out as if to steady myself, pressing one hand on his chest and the other on his belly. "Oops. Sorry, Tommy." Still under cover of trying to get my balance, I let my fingers scrabble a bit, just tickling lightly the center of his chest and the smooth flat area above his belly button. He reacted with a silent shout of breath, as if the last thing he expected was that I'd touch him in that way, and he was unprepared to keep secret the fact that he was…very ticklish.

Not panicking, acting as if everything was fine, he moved to sit up against the wall of the van. I sat and considered him there, barely visible in the light that came in through the bubble window over his head, sitting with his legs thrust out, crossed at the ankles. And I thought, *This is wrong.* It was so wrong to take advantage, to plot and scheme and work my suddenly sadistic will on an unsuspecting kid. And I didn't have to: I could stay where I was, not touching him, on the ride back to Kyle's house. But the *fact* of Tommy was also there—his long, nearly naked warm-skinned body, his mouth-watering vulnerability. Already my dick was hard, and in the blink of an eye *this is wrong* turned into *this is a fucking dream come true.* "Hey, Tommy," I rolled over toward him and let my hands scoot up his sides to find his ribs. He tried to twist away, but my fingers dug into him and the shock of it stopped him cold. I kept digging. His breath came in sharp little moans as I worked my fingers. "Ticklish, Tommy?" I asked, knowing that hearing the word "ticklish," confirming this was no accident, would make him feel even more helpless. Kyle was right: I did know what to do, and if Tommy hadn't caught on yet he would know shortly that I intended to tickle him till he was limp, barely breathing, and a cinch to get to Kyle's bedroom without a struggle.

Not that he didn't try to escape. For a minute or two he was all arms and legs, scrambling across the floor of the van, trying to fight me off, not shouting because he needed his breath to make those sharp moans that came ever more rapidly as I somehow kept my fingertips glued to his ribs. Then he kicked, and I grabbed his ankle and tickled the sole of his foot.

"Oh," he said, "oh, oh, oh." His other leg and his arms stopped moving and he sank back, immobilized by what I was making him feel. So I tickled him harder, burrowing into the sole of his foot. "Oh, oh, oh." He tried to struggle again, but I managed to swing his other leg around—already it was like handling a toy—

and trapped his ankles in the crook of my arm so I could tickle both feet at once.

Tommy's hands flapped weakly against the carpeted floor of the van, but that was all he could do—that, and shake his head back and forth as if trying to wake up from a bad dream. There was whispering now, mad whispering mixed in with his moans; and when he got wind enough to make his voice a little louder, I understood he was begging, begging me to stop. And I also understood, for the first time, how Kyle must have felt when he was tickling me and I was going *no, stop, don't!* and it only made him want to keep going harder, faster, tickling me till I was out of my mind.

After a while I let Tommy's overstimulated feet drop to the floor and went back to the rest of him, noticing on the way how the skimpy crotch of his swim trunks was even skimpier now that his hard-on pressed against it, threatening to burst out. I couldn't resist reaching, squeezing it through the cloth—"What you got there, Tommy?"—as my own cock, which had slowly been getting thicker, heavier, snapped to attention like a dog wakened by a cat. Except for Kyle, I had never touched another boy like this, and my head nearly exploded with the realization that there were so many boys in the world, so many cocks, so much ticklish skin....

Kyle turned a corner and again I fell onto Tommy, letting our crotches rub together. He was so weakened he could hardly move, and I set my hands free to torment his ticklish ribs. His reactions cycled from laughing to moaning to begging me to stop; when I dug my fingers into his armpits, his nearly breathless laughter rose to a hysterical pitch.

By the time Kyle pulled into his driveway Tommy was long past struggling. Drenched in sweat, panting heavily, and so sensitized that the touch of one finger brought his breathless laughter again, he was ours. My only question was, how would we get him into the house and upstairs?

Kyle opened the rear door and the bright afternoon sun poured in. I imagined eyes at every window of every house in the neighborhood. "Get him over here," he said.

I got my hands under Tommy's arms and tried to raise him. Nothing doing until I tickled his armpits, which got him moving, crawling with his last ounce of strength toward the open door as if it meant escape. When he got close enough, Kyle put his arms around him, just above his waist, and *heaved*. In a second Tommy was slung over Kyle's shoulder, Kyle turning toward the back door as if he were carrying nothing more than a ten-pound sack of potatoes. I ran ahead of him to get the door. Inside, at the foot of the stairs, Kyle looked at me, nodded his head toward Tommy's red trunks, which were just below his left shoulder, and said, "Pull 'em off." I grabbed the waistband of the trunks and pulled, sliding them down over Tommy's legs and limp feet. His ass was whiter than the rest of him, so much so that it seemed to glow in the dim light of the hallway. Kyle clapped a big brown hand over that ass, turned, and headed upstairs.

Kyle tied Tommy's wrists and ankles to the four-poster bed. The boy's long, hard dick lay against his belly. He couldn't speak, and his eyes stared without seeming to know what they were looking at. Kyle talked to him, though, as if they were having a conversation. "Ever been tied up before, Tommy?" he asked, stripping off his t-shirt. "Bet you've never been tied up naked with your dick all hard like that." Kyle pulled his shorts down, freeing his own hard-on to point at the ceiling. "We've got you right where we want you, buddy." He climbed up on the bed now, kneeling beside Tommy, running his fingertips across Tommy's chest, then letting them slide into Tommy's armpits. Within seconds Tommy was hysterical, shrieking in a voice so hoarse it sounded barely human. I didn't need any prompting, I reached for his nearest foot. I didn't know what would happen if we both tickled him at the same time, but I knew what I hoped would happen: I hoped that Tommy would *explode*. And what a thrill it was when I felt the surge go through him, the added torment of what I was doing to his feet. I knelt on the floor and used my tongue on Tommy's right foot, licking the sole, sucking the toes, tasting salt and sand. Nibbling on the arch, scratching my teeth across the ball. Bending the toes back with one hand, tautening the sole with my other so I could tickle it more effectively. Then I moved to his left foot and tickled, sucked, and nibbled till my legs ached from crouching on the floor.

I stood up, staggered back. My dick was so hard that unbuttoning and unzipping my cutoffs was a delicate operation. I kicked the shorts free and pulled off my t-shirt. Kyle was still intent on tickling Tommy's armpits, ribs, sides, and belly. I could hear the high-pitched keening sounds our victim made but couldn't see any part of him above the knees, just Kyle's broad laboring back and arms.

That was when a curious lifeless feeling came over me. At first I thought I was just tired, I needed to rest for a minute. I went to Kyle's desk and sat in his leather chair, careful not to let my cheeks spread where I might leave a stain. This gave me a different view of the bed: I saw Tommy's agonized grin as he turned his head from side to side, and Kyle's face in profile, his lower lip slack, a strand of saliva leaking down his chin to Tommy's chest. I looked away, my legs growing cold, my hard-on withering, something like nausea rising in my gut. Of course I knew what it was, though I had never felt it before, not like this:

I was *jealous*. A laugh escaped me as I thought of telling Kyle I was jealous of him and Tommy. I shook my head at the insanity of it, but I couldn't stop watching the two of them, and soon I was shaking my head in denial, not wanting to believe what I was seeing.

Tommy was panting hard, and so was Kyle, his dick drooling more than his mouth. The need to come was like static in the room, charging the air itself. Stupefied with lust, Kyle managed to be somewhat graceful in backing away from Tommy and off the bed. He untied Tommy's ankles. Tommy bent his knees enough to rest his soles on the bedspread. Then—this was where I began to get a kind of disembodied feeling, as if I were an unseen observing consciousness—Tommy bent his knees farther and lifted his legs, raising up his white ass, which got raised even higher as Kyle worked a pillow under it. Then he took each of Tommy's ankles and braced them on his shoulders. With his wrists still tied to the bedposts, Tommy was just as helpless as before, with one difference: he was now a fuck-toy. Kyle lost no more time in taking his slick cock in hand and fitting the tip to Tommy's asshole. With one bed-shaking thrust he was in, and with his hands on Tommy's legs he was thrusting again and again, all of his strength clenching in his buttocks and thighs as Tommy rocked back and forth, his arms immobile but his lower body workable, bendable, fuckable.

Despite the charged air in the room my skin felt colder, drier. I shivered with the knowledge that nothing that day had happened at random—Kyle had tied and fucked Tommy before. Feeling as removed from the scene as if I were watching it on TV, I put my shorts and T-shirt on and left Kyle's bedroom for the last time. For what had seemed like forever, all my thoughts and feelings had been directed toward him, while his thoughts and feelings had been no one's exclusive property. "This is wrong," I said over and over as I walked home, sick with the knowledge that, as impossible as it would have seemed earlier that day, Kyle would now be able to pass me on the street without even glancing in my direction. And I knew everything might have been different if, when my mind had formed the words *this is wrong* in the back of the van, I had paid more attention.

And so it was now. The course of our future depended on my ability to say *This is wrong* and make it stick.

Vega reached up, picked at a corner of the duct tape over Michael Loomis's mouth, and looked back at Sirius. "Can I?"

"Go ahead," Sirius said.

"Yeah," Pollux said. "We want to hear him beg for mercy."

Vega tore the tape off with a short, sharp pull to make it hurt as little as possible: the last courtesy Michael would ever know. Leering into the captive's face, Vega mocked him with those words that we had all heard, far too often: "Oh, my friend."

Recovered from his eye-rolling panic, Michael looked at us, curling his parched lips—looked us up and down and into the ground. Was he going to speak? We held our breath. Even the normal sounds of our surroundings—the creaking and crumbling of the decaying building, the scuttling of mice through the ruins—seemed to stop.

"This is wrong," I whispered again. Yet my resolve was melting. While the voice of conscience told me to wait, another voice spoke up to say Sirius was right: fuck being scared.

Then there was Michael's voice, which he finally found, summoning it up as a low, dry growl. "Do your worst," he said, and looked at each of us in turn as we shifted our weight, softly moaning or gasping in spite of ourselves. His voice had brought another dimension to him; no longer mute as a distant memory, he was *the real thing*, an achingly vulnerable beast who could be made to howl with torment, scream until the walls collapsed.

B lost no more time. He ran his fingers lightly, teasingly up and down the sole of Michael's right foot. Instantly Michael grimaced, clenching his teeth, shaking his head wildly.

More moans, surprisingly similar—a collective moan rising like our cocks, greeting the challenge to come. *This is wrong,* I thought, but this time it only skipped through my mind like a stone, barely making a splash. The truth was that I could no more resist Michael than I could have resisted Tommy Hatch on that long-ago Saturday. The only one of us who could resist Michael was Arcturus, who stood back, still wearing his coverall, watching as B tickled our captive's foot.

Scowling, whipping his head back and forth as his face turned red, Michael was revealing the exact opposite of what he intended—not toughness but vulnerability, the fact that he could be broken in minutes, perhaps even seconds. Things were happening very fast, from the split second when several of our hands landed on him to the moment when the force of our ravenous fingers became too much, his face split open like something overripe and he began to howl. I had been lucky enough to latch onto his left armpit, slick with sweat, its dark hairy eye gaping at me. To explore it fully, to coax every last sensation out of those few square inches of flesh, would take a lifetime, but I'd do what I could with the time I had left. Using my fingers and tongue on this quivering, salty prize became my religion, vocation, and avocation. When I glanced away, foaming at the mouth, to glimpse what the others were doing, it was too much to take in. Had any of the orgies in the Compound been as hungry as this one? As single-mindedly insane as our captors had been, had their hands ever sought so desperately to drive a man mad with sensation? Vega had buried his face in Michael's belly, his fingers in his sides. Pollux was as devoted to his ribs as I was to his armpit. Sirius was at his other armpit, and Polaris and Betelgeuse each had a foot. Then—time skipping again—there were bouts of free-for-all, each of us nose-diving toward some part of him we hadn't touched or licked yet. I slavered shamelessly over his thighs, making them twitch, making them tell me where the most sensitive spots were so I could move in with my beard and tongue and set up shop, hang up my shingle—24-HOUR THIGH TICKLING—and take up this new calling as devotedly as I had the old one.

But even that was not enough. I had to have all of him, and eventually I did. Fingering his feet, sucking on his toes, playing human fly on his heaving ribs. I took lessons from Vega on navel torture, he showed me how to use my tongue to get the most devastating results. Watching, B couldn't control himself any longer; he took his fine black cock in hand and, after a few strokes, shot thick streams of cum all over that ticklish belly. It was only the first cum-soaking as each of us, in turn, pulled himself off. By the time we were through, our prisoner looked like some kind of drenched insect pod, a slick and gleaming chrysalis. Beyond listening to his shrieking, none of us gave detailed attention to his distress; it was enough just to know it was there, that he was as ticklish as any of us and just as tortured as we had been. Panting, we took a moment now to examine him more closely. His chest and belly worked furiously as he gulped air, trying to make up for an intolerable stretch of breathlessness. His head still tossed from side to side, his eyes rolling. After a minute his labored breathing began to slow down, and other sounds began—not laughter, because he was way past that stage; more like the dysfunctional sounds of a poor recording, pops and pips and sprazzes from his overworked vocal cords, rasping stretches of static—the best he could do at pleading for us to let him go.

"He's not *totally* broken yet," Sirius said. "That's great. The best is yet to come." Like the rest of us, he was drenched with sweat and quite thirsty. With our shaking hands we broke out the water supply, trying in our lust-crazed state to remember we had to be careful, couldn't drink gallons the way we wanted to. In spite of our crazy twitching hands, we managed not to spill more than a drop. We even managed to give some to our prisoner, who sucked a cupful dry, easing some of the sounds coming from his throat. The next act of our play had not even begun, though. Now that he was covered in cum, we could play all kinds of slick, sloppy games on his ticklish skin. Personally, I always enjoyed sucking cum out of a man's fur. The armpit I'd devoted my life to earlier was now a saltier, spicier reservoir. We licked and sucked cum like starving puppies while letting our fingers roam at will. After a prolonged period of nearly silent squealing, our guest was reduced to more panting. We paused a moment and looked at him, nothing more than a bloated sac of consciousness sucking up oxygen. But was he broken yet? Not totally. I looked around at the others and saw that they agreed, and how wonderful that was--the telepathy shared by men on the same erotic journey.

We began the last act by tying off his balls with a cord and tickling them with our gauze "feathers." The reaction was more than we had hoped for from a man who was barely alive: his eyes rolled up farther into his head, his agonized grin widened, and a hysterical, crone-like *hee-hee-hee-hee* escaped from his lips. Encouraged, we tickled his balls for a long time, then untied his ankles so we could pull his legs back and tickle his asshole.

That was when the temptation finally became too strong for Arcturus, who had been standing behind us all that time, watching. Now he burst through our circle to pounce on Michael like a huge jungle cat, and we couldn't have been more surprised if a genuine wild animal had suddenly appeared. Most of us had never even seen him naked before, and now here he was, this *beast*, ripped and furred, with breathtaking thighs and a cock so thick and hard that no force on earth, let alone a half-decayed coverall, could have contained it. With B and Sirius holding Michael's legs up, Arcturus got to work, using his tongue on that exposed asshole while his fingers tormented our captive's highly sensitized scrotum. This got another great reaction, more nearly breathless hysteria that lasted and lasted until there was no doubt he'd finally lost his mind.

That was when Arcturus made his next move, relieving B and Sirius of Michael's legs, propping them up on his own shoulders as if they were no more than pick-up sticks. Before we knew it, his enormous dick had entered Michael's well-lubricated asshole, and we witnessed, over the course of what seemed like hours, an event that Sirius soberly described as "a fucking unto death."

When it was all over, we dragged Michael into the filthy hallway where the Lost Ones lived. "Here," Sirius said, releasing Michael's left arm as I let go of his right, letting him slump to the floor. "Here's some not-so-fresh meat for you guys."

One of the Lost Ones, the one I thought of as the shaggiest and ugliest, though in fact it was nearly impossible to tell them apart, stepped forward and prodded Michael with his foot. Only a soft moan indicated that the heap on the floor was actually alive. And exactly as if he were a piece of meat, the three wildmen fell on him, devouring him with their hands and mouths.

Sirius backed through the door and I followed. The sight of the Lost Ones falling on Michael...I had no more taste for ugly sights. But when someone shone a flashlight in our direction, and the glare forced me to turn away toward the reinforced glass of a sealed corridor door, I beheld the ugliest sight of all: my own reflection. No man, no *thing* crawling forth from the prehistoric ooze could have looked more abominable. So how much was there, after all, separating me from the Lost Ones? A thin thread of sanity? I nodded back in their direction and asked Sirius, "Who are they?"

He looked away. "They didn't make it as far as we did."

"They weren't trusties, like us?"

"No."

"Then what...?"

He reached out, placed a hand on my shoulder. "You really don't know the difference between us and them, do you?"

I shook my head, shook it as if to clear my mind, as if I knew what he was going to say next.

"We're the lost ones," he said. "Not them."

I wanted to know what he was talking about, but just then I stumbled—a wildly swinging flashlight beam was confusing me, robbing me of balance.

"Turn off that fucking light!" Sirius yelled.

But the flashlight stayed on, poking into the darkness, seeking the immediate corners of our existence; and someone—it might have been Pollux or Arcturus—spoke up in a voice that was frightened and accusing: "Where's Polaris?"

***

After a long period of confusion, panicky movements, and a suicidal waste of flashlight batteries, we came together to try to get our minds to work. Polaris *had* returned with us from the supply run; I remembered him standing among us as we contemplated

Michael Loomis, how he had said "What is it *now?*" when I had asked the group, foolishly, to wait. How his eyes had blazed with anger. The others remembered it too. But where he went after that…and when, and why….

Vega was at his most manic. "We've got to get *out* of here!"

"Calm down," I told him. "Don't get all worked up. It isn't going to help."

"But this is just part of their plan! Don't you see?"

"You're not helping."

"They're going to pick us off, one by one!"

I pushed him up against a wall and pressed my flashlight against his windpipe. "If that's true, there's not much we can do about it. Unless you've got a plan."

"My plan," he said in a half-choked voice, "Is to *get the hell out of here*. We can go deeper, much deeper into this place. Why wait one more fucking minute?"

"Pipe down," Pollux said, growling the way he used to do, when he was T-49. "Put a tampon in it, for Christ's sake."

We were standing by the door to the supply room. Having searched its meager space to make absolutely sure Polaris hadn't gone mad and was hiding in a corner, we were trying not to face the fact that we would have to leave the safe area to look for him.

"We'll do it like we do the supply run," Sirius said, "in twos."

"Why the fuck would he go back out there?" B asked.

"We don't know why. What do you suggest, *not* looking for him?"

B voted with his feet, backing away from the rest of us. "I ain't goin' out there," he said. "I can't."

Arcturus wagged his shaggy head. "I wish Rigel was here. He'd know what to do."

"Look," Sirius said, "we don't all have to go."

"I'll go with you," I said to him. "You and me." It wasn't bravery that inspired me, but restlessness: I'd go mad if I didn't do *something*.

We moved out, hands clasped, into the corridor. The treacherous path of the supply run stretched ahead as usual, except that the gaps in the floor, the dust and the darkness seemed more sinister than usual. It was tempting to think Polaris might have just strayed from the group to have some quiet time; we might find him sitting up against a wall, dozing. But a sweep of our flashlights across the broken plaster and masonry revealed nothing. We aimed our beams downward, looking into the gaps. There was nothing to see but dust particles swirling, but we were determined to look anyway.

"Careful," Sirius whispered. "Don't get too close to the edge."

"Okay." We were whispering for no reason except the darkness was full of tiny sounds that seemed to speak to us in code. Cracklings, indistinct voices, the wordless conversations of rats, the petulant moans of decay. If I listened, listened very hard, I could half-believe I heard crazed laughter coming from Dred Junior's cell, could even hear my own insane cries issuing from a tape player. "That way madness lies," I whispered, and when Sirius looked at me, questioning, I shook my head. "Nothing."

Cautiously I got down on the floor, crept toward the edge of the nearest hole. It was the hole where Rigel went down. I was determined to see *something* down there. It was dangerous, all right, the floor around the hole creaking as I inched forward. When I was close enough I plunged my head and right arm through the hole, aimed the flashlight beam directly below me. Through the cloud of dust I saw, incredibly, the flash of another light—someone aiming a flashlight up from at least fifty feet below. It took me several seconds to realize I was seeing, not another light, but a reflection of my own, the quality of the image—sharp, yet slightly out of register—suggesting water. Reaching with my free hand, I found a piece of broken tile and pushed it over. The reflection shattered as the tile landed, disappearing with barely a sound. So this was—what? No mere flooded subbasement, no amalgam of slop-bucket sewage. With nothing to go on I sensed the depth and volume of something greater, something older—an underground river? It was a grave, for certain—for anyone unlucky enough to fall into it.

I crept back, carefully but quickly, haunted by the sight of that unknown water. A wave of dread passed over me, making me shiver to the bone. It was all I could do to get to my feet without falling over. "Sirius?" I called, intending to tell him what I had seen. When he wasn't in immediate range of my light I looked farther, sweeping the beam down the corridor as if he had struck out ahead, which was … unlikely. The secret to survival was staying close. He knew that. "Sirius?"

Instead of moving forward I retraced my steps; surely he was behind me, he had not gone on ahead. The holes in the floor seemed to have shifted positions again. I had a new puzzle to figure out as I crossed this rotting landscape that would never, no matter how many times I crossed it, become familiar.

When it was clear—pitilessly clear, like the reflection of strong light in water—that Sirius was gone, gone for good, I raised my head and howled.

***

We all sat waiting—waiting for a sign from Sirius, or for someone among us to speak a brave word. But when someone did speak it was Vega, uttering the secret fear we all shared.

"We'll never get out of here," he said.

"Shut up," B said.

"No, it's all right," I said. "Someone had to say it. We're all thinking it."

"Well," Pollux said, "if we're going to get out of here, it will have to be soon."

"There's nothing to worry about," B said. "Dogface took a wrong step in the dark, and he fell. That's all there is to it. It could have happened to anybody."

"And Polaris? He took a wrong step, too?"

The debate raged on: when should we try to escape? Vega, having just said we'd never get out, began his sing-song about how we had to leave *now*.

"I say we stay right here," Pollux said.

"That's right," B said. "All we can do is wait till the next supply run. If Sirius hasn't shown up by then, we'll tell them. We'll tell them, and they'll tell us what to do."

"Wait," I said. "Wait, wait, wait." A sudden attack of light-headedness took my feet right out from under me, I sank to the floor. "Wait, wait, wait."

B put his hand on my shoulder. "You all right?"

A bubble of laughter rose in my windpipe. I had to let it out, I couldn't help it. But once it came, it wouldn't stop. Sitting on the floor, rocking back and forth, I was helpless with laughter.

"He's fucking lost it," Pollux said.

"No, no," I said, wiping tears from my eyes. "It's just that…he said wait till it's time for the supply run…."

"So what?"

"So…." I was off again. It was another minute before I could speak. "So…we wait till it's time. But *where is the time*?"

"You mean…."

"Oh *fuck*," B said.

"That's right, that's right," I said, still rocking back and forth, seeking a comfort that wouldn't come. "When Sirius went, he took the time with him."

Perhaps we all had the same image in our minds at that moment: the tiny face, smaller than a dime, of the woman's wristwatch that Sirius always carried in his coverall pocket. Surely we could all picture it—its minuscule hands, its tiny hatch marks in place of numerals. Its sheer *unwillingness* to tell the time clearly and forcefully. It was all we had, and now it was gone.

"We're fucked," Pollux said.

"Naw, man," B said. "We can't give up."

"*Think* about it." Pollux backed B up against the wall, driving one finger into his chest. "When is the next supply run? Tomorrow? And when is that? Do you even know if it's day or night? I sure as hell don't. He...*kept track*."

Laughing no more, I sat shaking my head, unable to fathom the sadness of our situation. We should have had a backup system, another way of marking the hours and days. We should have worked to make our safe place safer, the corridor less treacherous. If only we had been in our right minds to begin with, it might have happened, it might have worked. If only Rigel were here—yes, I was falling into that pattern of thought also, and I hadn't even known the man. But it didn't matter, because Rigel went down.

Vega was muttering again. "We've got to get out of here, we've got to get out of here...."

"We've got to rest," I said. I couldn't keep my eyes open, could barely raise my head. "We've got to rest. Then we'll try." I left it to the others to put out the candles, check the supply room door, take a last look around. I fell asleep where I was, sitting up against the wall.

I woke up, not knowing where I was or how to account for a darkness so absolute it seemed to be pressing against me. It was the darkness of the grave, and again I had to wonder if I might be dead. Reaching out, my hand touched skin. A hand slid over mine. B. He was the cure for the darkness. I buried my face in his chest, let tears gather there as he stroked my filthy hair. I held on to him and rocked. In this complete oblivion my body was as much his as it was mine. I wrapped my legs around him, felt him growing hard. This intimacy, this gentle rocking together in the dark—I'd never felt so close to a man. If he'd only asked, I would have shed my skin then and there, reconfigured myself into whatever would give him comfort. As it was I sensed some regrouping inside of me—a new accommodation, an openness. Silently, using my hands, I told him what to do. We tumbled into place. Lying on my back, my legs on his shoulders, I had another spell of light-headedness: I was not lying on a floor but suspended in midair.

His immensity moved against me. A dry searing pain wouldn't be denied. It swung me on its axis until, sitting upright in the dark, fully impaled, I pitched my fear headlong into a far corner of the universe. Then I sped off in a new direction, riding through the sky with my mouth open, no longer a lonely, disconnected consciousness but a force of creation, blazing through pitch darkness like a star.

3. THE ATTEMPT

I woke up rocking gently along the length of my spine. B had put a motion in me that wouldn't quit. Put another way, he had fucked me all night, way past the point where another man would have quit from sheer exhaustion. Rolling over now, I laid my hands on his warm back, my lips between his shoulder blades. He moaned, softly, and I got closer, spooning my legs against his, pressing my soft dick into the crack of his ass. For the first time, I felt it wouldn't be bad if it turned out I *was* dead, if this was what it was like.

But the general shifting and turning of bodies around me told me this wasn't death, this was morning—or what passed for morning. Two hands slid around my ankles, and I realized Pollux had been sleeping at my feet. "Hey, help me out," he said softly, and I let him pull on my ankles, arrange the soles of my feet against either side of his massive hard-on. Meanwhile I let my hands tickle gently across B's back.

"Hey, lay still," he said.

"Can't. I'm getting my feet fucked." Tickling more aggressively, I moved to his ribs, what I could reach of them with him lying on his side. He took a sharp breath, then several sharp breaths, and I understood the erotic state he was entering and wanted to take him all the way into it. I found his lower ribs, the spots where, he had told me once, he could be tickled to death some day—a lie, a desperate move to protect his terminally ticklish feet. His body stiffened, his back arched, but he could not pull away--no more than I could pull away from the use my bare soles were being put to, rubbing against a slick hot cock. Judging by the sounds Pollux was making, it was a good fuck for him too.

Suddenly Vega's voice piped up: "Somebody'd better either fuck me or suck me."

"C'mere," I said. Temporarily leaving B, I rolled over onto my back, rotating my feet around the big cock fucking them. Vega's hairy thighs straddled me, and his fingers sought my lips so he could guide his cock between them. Despite the moans and yelps rising in me as Pollux slammed into my feet, I kept focused on Vega, giving him a tight juicy blow, my involuntary bursts of breath only increasing his sensations. Meanwhile B rolled up against my side to press his stiff dick into the tender hollow below my ribs, the spot where I'd just been tickling him. At the same time his huge hand closed over my shaft and stroked. Like most of our clusterfucks it was unplanned, improvised, threatening to shudder apart any second; it was also as intense as it could get, especially when Pollux and Vega both came at the same time, cum exploding against my soles and the roof of my mouth. Then Vega rolled off me, or possibly I threw him off with my squirming, for Pollux was licking my feet dry, his rough tongue bringing tears to my eyes as B continued to jack me off slowly, persistently while tickling my side with his hard-on. In my delirium I felt time stand still till I finally came—my fourth or fifth orgasm since I'd started counting sometime during the night.

B hadn't come yet. I wondered if he was ready for me again, and got my answer as he kneeled between my legs and placed them up on his shoulders. He entered me quickly and my asshole closed around him like an old friend's handshake. The tireless fucking he'd given me had birthed and nurtured an intimacy that let me say, as I'd never been able to say to a man before, "My ass belongs to you."

When he was finished and I had his warm load, he rolled onto his back again, perhaps thinking he was going to get a few minutes' rest. But my fingers were restless, wanting to climb over his hairy torso and find the depths of his armpits. "No, no, no," he moaned—more ticklish, as usual, after coming. His begging only made me tickle him more. Vega and Pollux were getting into it too, Pollux as usual busying himself with B's huge tender feet while Vega tickled his thighs and balls. Once B settled into a steady, desperate panting we made sure to keep him there. Dark as it was, I had to imagine his mouth gaping open, his eyes rolling, his fingers scrabbling weakly against the floor. Vega moved up, from his groin to his superticklish belly, and I moved down, from his armpits to his upper ribs. The way his body shook and rocked, I figured Pollux was having another foot-fuck.

How long did that four-way play last? When it was over I only knew that it must have been hours. I had fucked Vega, Pollux had taken B up the ass, and I had so much cum in my throat that it took several swallows of our precious water to wash it down. It was the water that brought me back to the reality of our immediate future: we had to get out of here. Sure enough, as soon as I said the words to myself Vega took up the mantra and wouldn't stop: "We've got to get out of here, out of here, out of here…."

"Shut up already," I told him. Something was eating at me, a dread that by now had become familiar. "Oh Jesus, where's Arcturus?"

Even in the uncertain light Pollux looked pale. "Wasn't he here? He's always here, somewhere."

It gripped us more strongly than ever—the fear, the dread. The usual litany of questions—*Who saw him last? Who spoke to him last? Who, who, who?*—yielded the usual results.

"He kept to himself so much of the time," Vega said quietly. I was so used to his panicky whining that to hear him suddenly speak in a tone of nostalgia, as if he were growing used to loss, scared me to death.

"We should have accounted for everyone," Pollux said, "before we started fucking and sucking." It was his old anger surfacing, aimed more at himself than anyone else.

"Take it easy, for Chrissake." Arcturus shone his flashlight down from above, by the supply room door. "While you guys were having a circle jerk, I've been trying to get our shit together."

He'd gotten some food ready for us, the last of the previous supply run's bread divided into small plastic bags labeled, with an irony we were used to by now, BIOHAZARD. He had dressed, and our filthy coveralls and boots were waiting for us too. Putting on that stiff cloth was like trying to dress in cardboard, but we had no choice.

***

B, his voice still hoarse from the tickling we'd given him, said to me, "I've gotta show you all something. Something Rigel showed me once. I forgot about it, but sometime during the night I remembered."

I followed him, carrying a candle. He held a flashlight, and aimed it at the wall next to the supply room door. "Hold it here just like this," he said. He began to dig at the wall with his fingers. A hairline crack appeared between two cinder blocks, and began to widen. Soon he was able to work a block free enough to slide it partly out. The whole wall was a goner, you could see it crumbling into dust someday; for now it held up as B reached in and pulled out a brown envelope. "Crystal gave this to Rigel soon after he came down here."

He handed it to me. The flap was only partly sealed. I tore it loose and pulled out a yellow sheet with feminine handwriting on it:

DIRECTIONS OUT - TO USE IN CASE OF EMERGENCY

*If something happens and we're not here to help you, leave AS SOON
AS YOU CAN. Do NOT try to leave the way you came, up the
stairwell. Use the supply route instead, up to the next level ONLY and
head south. We're preparing a way.*

"This is it?" I asked. "This is all we have?"

"Hey, it may be enough."

Pollux was reading over my shoulder. "Shit," he said. "Just tell me one thing, where the fuck is 'south'?"

I covered my mouth to hide a laugh, but it broke loose anyway, briefly climbing to a hysterical pitch. It was true: in her life-saving instructions for us, Crystal had miscalculated. She lived in a world where everyone had a sense of direction, maybe even a compass, and a watch, and a switch somewhere to turn on a light. Not to mention soap, and hot water, and toothpaste, and heating and cooling, and shoes that fit, and comfortable clothes.

"It's all we've got," B said. "We've gotta try."

"Wait," Pollux said. "What do we do about…them?"

The Lost Ones, he meant. Which also meant Michael. Now I noticed what I should have noticed earlier—they weren't making any noise. It was time to bring them some food and water anyway, so we got some provisions from the supply room and headed down the dusty aisle to the side corridor.

The Lost Ones were gone. Only Michael Loomis lay there, unconscious, in the grip of a nightmare, his chest heaving, head twisting from side to side.

"Where the fuck are they?" Pollux asked.

"They couldn't've got far," B said.

"The hell they couldn't." Pollux headed for the door to the stairwell and found it standing partly open—we never left it that way. "Quiet," he said, motioning for us to follow him. The stairwell, stretching above us, so still and menacing, was dim in what little light leaked down, yet blindingly bright compared to our cave. He led us up the two half-flights that had brought us down here. The door to the corridor we'd entered from was partly open also. Impossible. Pollux reached for the door handle, and something like a scream rose in me, a shrill warning, *don't, don't open it.* But he was only pulling it closed, just as he closed the door at the bottom of the stairwell behind us when we returned. The Lost Ones had fled, choosing a route that was, according to Crystal's note, the most dangerous. But they didn't know any other, and who knew, after all, how much choice their poor minds were capable of. They could easily have taken off in a blind panic, frightened by their own fear into a flight that stood no chance.

I asked Pollux, "Do you know what Sirius meant, when he told me once that we were the lost ones, not them?"

"No," he said, taking a beat too long to answer.

I didn't press it. Instead I turned my flashlight on Michael again, and this time it was enough to wake him. He coughed and sputtered as if I'd poured a cupful of water on his face. "We're getting out of here," I said, "and we're taking you with us." Behind me, Pollux breathed a protest—*oh fuck no*—but I could see that Michael was too far gone to be of any harm. To prove it, I handed my flash to B and fit my hands over Michael's ribcage.

As I tickled him, his mouth stretched wide in a grin, his tongue appeared at the corner of his mouth, and his eyes rolled as if he were following a pinball game on the ceiling.

"Look at him," I said. "He's a total fucking goonybird."

"Oh, fuck, *no*," Pollux said again. "We ain't taking this fucker with us, hell no."

I stood up. "He won't do us any harm, and he might actually be some help. As a bargaining chip, or something."

It took some discussion, but we reached a compromise. On the slim chance that he *might* know something that would help us, Michael could come along. He would have to travel naked, because we had no coveralls for him; and Arcturus insisted that he have his wrists bound together and his mouth stuffed with gauze. Pollux remained the lone dissenter in our vote to take him along.

For once, no one pointed out that Rigel would have known what to do.

Arcturus and Pollux took the lead, then B and me, then Vega and Michael, who walked along obediently, no doubt lucid enough to know if he caused any trouble he'd be left behind, tickled to death, or both.

I could no longer look down this corridor without feeling my stomach clench like a fist. Remembering the last time I was here— was it just hours ago?—and saw my light reflected down below made me shake with fear. And our progress this time, perhaps because it was the last time, seemed so slow...so slow. When we finally reached the end I realized I had scarcely been breathing, and took in such a deep gulp of air I had a coughing fit from the dust in my lungs and throat.

Pollux took the makeshift steps up to the ceiling and hoisted himself through the trap door. Arcturus was next, then B, then

Vega. I struggled up the steps with Michael, and with the help of the men above, we pulled and pushed him through the hole. I took one last look around, one more sweep of my flashlight before I climbed through. It was the last time I would ever see this hallway—except perhaps in nightmares, if I survived to have any.

On the next level there was nothing significant in our flashlight beams, just another hallway like the one we had left, another decrepit tiled floor. Up ahead we would have a choice of turning left or right, with nothing but guesswork to go on. Pollux put an arm around Michael's throat and growled in his ear, "Do you know where we are?" Michael only wagged his head in confusion. Pollux reached two fingers into his mouth, pulled out the gauze, and tossed it aside. Still Michael was silent, as if the strand of drool leaking down his chin had tethered his tongue. Pollux turned his head and spat in disgust. "He *might've* been of use to us if we hadn't damn near killed him."

"Yeah," B said, "but he might have been a hell of a lot more dangerous too." He took a look for himself in Michael's frightened eyes, to see if there might be some knowledge there that would aid our escape, but it was no use. I was disappointed, but my hopes had not been high to begin with.

Still it was Michael who noticed something after all. I saw it in his face as his eyes followed a stray flashlight beam. He blinked and kept blinking, seemingly in surprise. Then he began to laugh. As much as we had heard him laugh, there was something new in his high-pitched cackling, a shrill note of triumph. Trip-wired as we were, he raised a panic that had me cursing at B.

"Turn your fucking light up there again, man! No, farther up."

B let his light climb the wall and follow the edge of the ceiling to the intersecting hallway.

Vega screamed. I tried to, felt it rising my throat, but it got lost in a wash of bitter bile. I doubled over, choking till there were tears in my eyes. When I straightened up I swung my flashlight past B, who was trembling—I could hear his teeth chattering—up to that corner of the hallway again. Pollux growled like a dog. None of us moved a step, we could only stare.

The security camera stared back, a tiny green light beneath its lens blinking and blinking.

Michael laughed on, hoarsely. Any of us could have killed him just to end the noise, but no one moved. I felt whatever hope I'd held onto leaching away from my body like a falling fever, leaving me weak, rooted to the floor.

Finally Arcturus said, "We can't just keep standing here."

"Well, where the fuck do we go?" B asked.

I swallowed, still trying to keep down the bitterness filling my throat. "Away," I said. "Away from here. Away from that fucking camera."

I took B's arm and backed away. Arcturus and Pollux and Vega followed. Only Michael didn't move. I couldn't take my eyes off that blinking green light till we were past the trap door, our backs against a wall.

"What do we do with him?" Pollux asked.

I didn't need to shine my light in his face to see his eyes drilling into Michael. I trained my light on the madman's white ass, then his slumped shoulders, which gave him the posture of a tired commuter waiting for a train. I saw easily enough what we could do: pull him over to the trap door and pitch him down head first, to break through the floor below into oblivion. It was so easy to see in my mind's eye that I replayed it again and again, heard his final scream of terror as he vanished from sight. But nothing like that was going to happen. I remembered his story of lying in a field while his cousins were tickling him, staring at a cloud and seeing a white ship that could take him away; and how, when his uncle and cousins were all tickling him, he first heard the voices that would continue to haunt him for the rest of his life. Now it was time to leave him alone. "Just leave him," I said. "If he follows us, fine. If not, who cares."

"Follows us?" Again Pollux turned his head and spat. "Where are we fucking going? For all we know they're already on their way here."

"Well, don't fucking look at me," I said. "I don't have the answer any more than you do."

Suddenly Arcturus turned and slammed his fist into the wall. "Rigel!" he hollered. "Rigel, where are you!"

For a minute or so we just stood there, shuffling our feet, our hands in our pockets. Invoking Rigel had brought back memories—even to me, though I'd never known him. But he was the first of us to go down, and if he hadn't then maybe everything else would have been different. We might not have lost Polaris and Sirius; we might even have managed to save the Lost Ones. Now we were all thinking, *Five of us left. Only five.*

Suddenly the ripping sound of a hastily pulled zipper made me flash my light to the left. There was Vega, his hard-on popping up from his coverall.

"Somebody's gonna have to jack me off," he said.

Pollux struck the wall with his beefy fist. "Jesus Christ, I don't fucking believe it!"

"Look, I'm nervous as hell, okay? All I'm asking for is a hand job."

Because keeping the peace, such as it was, seemed the most important thing, I moved up behind Vega, reached in front of him with my free hand and grabbed his dick. "The only good thing about him," I said, "is that he never takes very long." Sure enough, after about a dozen strokes he started to shudder. I heard his cum spatter the wall.

"Thanks," he said. "Sorry."

"You'd do the same for me, right?"

Instinctively I moved to the left, and the others followed. This hallway was more intact than the one below, the treacherous holes fewer and far between. Swinging my flashlight, I tried to look everywhere at once—up ahead, behind me, down at my panicked feet. I couldn't quite see where this path was taking us, and the suspense made me move even faster, praying for my light to find something, *anything*.

At last the end of the corridor appeared in my weakening beam. Getting closer, I saw a wall with some kind of hole in it. A doorway? No, if the irregular edges I saw held true.

"It's a dead end!" Pollux yelled.

"No!" I called back. "Come on!" The more I saw of that hole in the wall the more excited I felt. It was too small, too *deliberate-*looking to be the product of collapse or decay; round-shouldered, nearly flush with the floor, it gave every appearance of being a tunnel. Not a picnic to crawl through, but better than the tiny aluminum duct that had brought me here.

I waited for the others to catch up. We stood around the opening, which only came up to our waists. Playing our beams into it, we saw that the hole didn't lead into another room but into earth. It *was* a tunnel, and what else could it be but the way out that Crystal had referred to in her instructions? Still we stood, restlessly, shifting our weight, taking a step forward, a step back. We needed time to consider this; but there was no time, that was the agony of it.

"Me first," Pollux said. "If I can fit through there, you guys can, too."

"Careful," I told him, as if we had a choice whether to be careful or not. I was practically holding my breath as he crawled in, keeping his flashlight beam aimed before him.

It wasn't long before he called back, "Come on! This goes on for a ways."

I went next. The gray seat of Pollux's coveralls had holes in it, I could see his hairy ass poking through. Beyond that, and the soles of his boots, there wasn't much to see but brown crumbling dirt—a little too crumbling, for my taste, as if there might be a collapse any second; but again, what choice did we have? I looked behind to see B following me. "Vega's behind me," he said.

"Where's Arcturus?"

"He's keeping a lookout, just in case."

We were crawling less than a minute when Pollux started cussing.

"What is it?" I asked. I couldn't resist the urge to whisper, as if we might be overheard, even here.

"This looks like the end of it," he said.

"What are you up against? Is it solid earth?"

"No, a lot of loose dirt, like there's been a cave-in."

Sweat dripped into my eyes as I tried to think. Loose dirt could be dug away. But how much, for how long? And even then would it lead to a way out?

Finally Pollux said, "Let's go back."

With no room to even turn around, we had to shift into reverse. More than once Pollux's boot scraped my hand, and I accidentally kicked B in the face. By the time we hit floor tile again we were filthier than ever, tired and groaning with disappointment and disgust. I sank down with my back against a wall. "Somebody's gonna have to fuck me," I said, but it didn't get much of a laugh.

Craving rest, I closed my eyes.

"So what do we do now?" Pollux asked. After a long pause he added, "Christ, don't everybody speak at once."

Vega's trembling voice piped up. "Where's Arcturus?"

"Oh, shit...."

I opened my eyes. The horror was still with us; I saw it in the faces that turned toward mine, confirming that Arcturus wasn't where he should be. But we'd had the same concern earlier that day, before we'd even started out, and Arcturus had turned up in the supply room. He was surely not far away now, serving his duty as lookout. I closed my eyes....

"What do we do?" someone muttered.

Some time had passed—a minute, or several minutes. Flashlights blinked on and off like fireflies, beams reflecting off old green institutional paint, and I sensed a renewed anxiety level, as if everyone's nerve ends had been freshly doused with something toxic. No, Arcturus was *not* somewhere around; he was gone.

"What do we *do?*" It was Vega again, and I didn't need to see him to know he was wringing his hands.

"We make a run for it," Pollux said, "back the other way, through those double doors."

"Oh, shit, man," B said. "Right under that camera?"

"Well, if you or anybody else has a better idea, let's hear it."

No one said a word. I sensed the sagging of hearts and minds. That short crawl through the tunnel had been exhausting, and now to have Arcturus missing...who had the hope, the stamina for a prolonged flight?

"You guys," B said, "go on without me."

He was propped against the wall, too, not far from me. I scooted over and placed a hand on his shoulder. "What are you talking about?"

"I'll catch up." His eyes looked tired, his voice sounded even worse. "Go on."

"You think I'm going to leave you sitting here? No fucking way!"

He grabbed my upper arm, leaned into me. "They're on their way to get us right now, man. It's no fucking use."

"Listen to me." I shrugged him off. "We're not going anywhere without you, so get ready to move your ass."

"I'm finished, man. I'm finished."

"Turn on your flashlight."

He gave a laugh that had no life in it. "It's finished too."

"I want to see you get up and walk."

"Okay." He tried, levering himself forward, then sank back again.

"Come on." I tried to set an example by springing to my feet in one smooth move, but it wasn't too smooth--I had to catch myself with one hand against the wall. With the other I reached down to him. "Come on!"

With my help he got to his feet with a grunt, and took a few unsteady paces down the hall. I watched, aiming my light after him, and immediately saw something strange. An optical illusion, maybe, some trick of fatigue: he was leaving footprints on the ruined tile. Black footprints, as if he'd shucked his boots and his black skin were leaving its mark on the floor.

"Hold it," I said.

He crumpled to the floor.

Beneath that illusion of black footprints lay an awful truth that couldn't be denied as I kneeled by him, touched his left side, and felt his soaked torn coverall. He was wounded. I placed my hands on his shoulders. "What happened?"

"I don't know. Something sharp in that tunnel, somewhere in the dirt. Stuck me good."

"It's okay." Trying to assess the damage, trying not to hurt him, all I could find was torn cloth, torn flesh, blood sickeningly warm on my hand. "You'll be okay."

He shook his head. "I'm gone, man." He kept his voice soft, not out of weakness, but as if he wanted to make sure his wound was kept secret, something between him and me, the others not needing any more bad news right now.

"You guys all right?" Pollux moved toward us, his light sweeping the floor, and instinctively I shielded B's bad side. When Pollux and Vega saw their wounded friend, it wouldn't be what I saw. It wasn't just B lying there; it was my future, insofar as I dared to dream of such a thing—a life with B, of never being separated from him again. A life of total physical and emotional commitment, his skin pressed against mine for tens of thousands of nights. His eyes were so deep, there was so much more to know, so much more *time* I needed to stare into them.

Pollux stopped short, no doubt sensing that B and I were having a private moment. "Let's get going," he said, his flashlight beam averting us but playing anxiously against the wall.

"We're ready," I said, helping B to his feet, praying he'd make it this time. In spite of his soaked overalls and the bloody footprints on the floor, there had to be a chance that he wasn't hurt that bad after all. With my support he was able to walk, leaning his good side into me, swinging his right leg as I moved my left, as if we were paired for a three-legged race. I told the others, "You two go on. Run for it. We'll catch up."

Pollux and Vega also stood as one, joined at the hip, shaking their heads in unison. "No way," Pollux said. "We go together."

He and Vega took the lead, slowing their pace so that we could keep up, even though it made the corridor seem so much longer than it had before. After a while I thought we'd made a wrong turn, it couldn't be this long a walk back. B was sagging more and more, and again I heard him say, "I'm gone."

"Shut the fuck up."

"I'm gone, man."

Without thinking I used my free hand to grip his lower jaw and raise his face to mine. I kissed him, tasting so many things—tunnel dirt, metallic fear, even the salt-and-sweet of semen, residue from a thousand thrusts. I tasted what made him male, reveled in his rough tongue and chipped molar, ran my tongue-tip lovingly across his ticklish palate. I let go only when I feared I might be holding him too hard, might be on the verge of hurting him.

"I love you, Duke," I said.

As if I'd spoken a curse—the worst kind, that could set loose a chain reaction to wreck the world—I suddenly saw all that would *not* happen, the life that *would not* be, compared to what we'd had, these pathetic filthy days in an abandoned hole. *Help me,* I wanted to say, as if I were the one hurt after all, the one who would have to be propped up from this point on. *Help me, save me.*

B was struggling. Fighting for air, like a man near the end? No, thank God, only straining to get his lips closer to my ear. "I love you, too, Rand," he said.

If that didn't quite dispel the curse, at least it brought me back to the present. I held him and knew that all wasn't lost; there was hope. His chest expanded with each breath, his thighs held him up, and in his loins an old fire smoldered, still capable of sparking into flame.

"You'd damn well better live," I growled into his ear, "so you can fuck me again."

Vega and Pollux had gone ahead after all, no longer within range of my flashlight beam, weak as it was. Overcome by a sense that we had to *hurry*, yet knowing how impossible it was, I tried anyway to speed us up, to get our tiring legs moving just a bit faster…and faster. Amazingly B kept up, matching me step for step. There was exhilaration in his movement now, as if he saw something up ahead that I couldn't. Soon his strength exceeded mine, he slipped away from me to stride ahead, till he had a lead of several yards. "I heard something," he said.

"Wait up!" I called, trying to summon my own burst of strength. There was such a thing as a second wind and I called on it now, certain I could not only overtake the others but outdistance them, lead the way into our long-delayed escape. It would take more effort than I was putting out, though, for now even B was out of sight. A sudden stitch in my side made me stop, lean my hand against the wall. I turned my flashlight off to save a few seconds' worth of batteries, and took a mental inventory of the shape I was in. Just slightly winded, that was all. But tuning into my inner body and assessing the damage of fear and stress had dulled my outer senses, so I wasn't tracking any signs of movement, any noises that might have warned me of what I'd see when I turned my flashlight on again.

Michael Loomis stood just inches in front of me. His hands, free of the cords that had once bound them tightly, grasped a length of pipe that he had raised above his head, and were a split second away from bringing it down on me.

I threw myself backward, landing hard on my tailbone and rolling to the side—avoiding the pipe, I hoped, even as I comprehended the silence I lay in, as total as the darkness. Surely there was no Michael, no pipe, just a fevered imagination that had spent too long in the dark.

The pipe hit right beside me, taking a chunk out of the floor.

Jumping up, flashing my light enough to glimpse Michael's midsection moving toward me, I threw myself forward this time, desperately trying to maintain a grip on the flashlight as I tackled him and we both fell hard, too hard for a floor that hadn't been touched for too long by anything but dust. I managed to get to my hands and knees just as the cracking and groaning caught up with me--then there was nothing holding me up anymore. I was hanging with my fingers clutching a broken edge as the rest of me dangled above—what? I clenched my teeth, tried to lift myself but didn't have the strength. Nor did I have the strength to hold on much longer. Twist my head as I might, there was nothing to see but darkness, my flashlight a thing of the past. I tried to speak, found my throat full of dust and tried again, even though the effort seemed to leach all strength from my fingers.

"Help," I called, a pathetic sound in the suffocating dark. "Help!"

"Oh, my friend…."

I had hoped against hope that Michael had fallen, had vanished as if he really had been an illusion all along. Now there was his voice, right above me, and I felt something of the helplessness I'd known as his prisoner at his farmhouse.

"Oh, my friend," he said now, "no use calling for help. I just killed your Black pal, just like I killed the others. There's only you now, and you're going fast." His voice seemed to come from directly above me, and that was confirmed when the weight of his bare foot pressed on my fingertips. A boot would have been crueler, but this was enough to make me yell again. How much longer could I hold on? No use trying to measure it in seconds. The time I had left was shorter than that.

Then came the sound of something ripe splitting open, and the weight that pressed intolerably on my fingers gave one last knuckle-crushing push and was gone, a heavy weight falling past me in the darkness, nearly dragging me with it. My fingers still held on, not by virtue of strength but of fear. They were too paralyzed to let go. Which wouldn't keep the crumbling floor from winning after all, its creaking and cracking dislodging a stream of dust that ran down my nose. The unknown, tired of waiting for me, was about to grab my ankles and pull me down to my doom.

What came instead was a firm grip, not on my ankles but on my nearly numb wrist, the shock of it making me cry out. Oh Christ, it wasn't Michael that had fallen past me in the dark--the madman was still with me.

Or...?

"Easy, easy," said a voice that was *not* Michael's. It was B, pulling me up slowly, painfully over the floor's broken lip. Scraped and bleeding, I was at least on a level enough surface to crawl to safety. Once I stopped feeling the bottomless pit nipping at my heels, I wanted to speak, to breathe B's name, but all I could do was gulp air and hope that the beating of my heart, which had been in overdrive for some time, would settle down before it gave out.

"It's all right," he was saying, "it's all right, it's all right." Though I could see well enough how it wasn't, as I turned my head and saw his weak flashlight beam glowing on his blood-soaked thigh, which looked more ghastly than before in the dangerously dimming light.

"He said he'd killed you," I said finally.

"He killed Arcturus. That was the noise I heard, the big guy dying back there, his head split open. Sorry I left you. Come on, now."

I was hurting where I'd scraped against the floor, but my wounds were nothing compared to his. Which made it more of a miracle that he could have saved me at all and could still help me now, pulling me up by my aching arm, brushing debris from my coverall with a gentle hand. He even took the lead as we headed off, his faltering light our guide along the floor that seemed more treacherous than ever now that I knew what it was like to fall through it, to dangle helplessly in the dust. Any doubt I'd be doomed without him vanished when I realized how my short-term memory had vanished too; I no longer seemed to know where I was or where we were headed. Not until we saw the faint blinking green of the surveillance camera did I remember our chance-in-hell plan of bullying our way out, past that hateful camera, through the double doors. Slowly, quietly, nearly holding our breath, we moved on. Pushing those doors open was an effort, we had to stop for a second and catch our breath—down another hellishly long hallway, my lungs burning with effort, B moaning with each tortured step, finally through another doorway into the stairwell Crystal had warned against returning to; I didn't care. That blessed, natural light leaking down from above was to my eyes what water would have been to my parched throat, and when I looked up to the next landing there were Pollux and Vega, sitting side by side, their hands on their knees, like workers taking a break. They didn't speak, and when I got close enough I could see the astonishment on their faces, as if I were a ghost. A freaky, uncontrollable grin split my face as I hauled myself up and past them, croaking out, "Come on, what are you waiting for?"

A few more half flights and we were on the same level as the daylight, streaming so strongly through the glass bricks surrounding this final door that, unless my deprived eyes could no longer gauge such things, it had to be midday outside. Not knowing what I would find upon pushing open this door made me hesitate for a second. Nothing could be worse than the prospect of having to return the way we'd just come, because we would not, could not make that trip again, wouldn't last beyond the bottom of the stairwell. When I finally did push open the door, the bright strip of ground and grass and blue sky brought tears to my eyes. Vega, then Pollux, then finally B pressed through the doorway after me.

We were in an open passageway, an alley between two wings of the building. I picked up my aching feet and pushed myself forward, concentrating on the calm strip of grass ahead, praying it wasn't an illusion. "Free," I said, trying out the word, not daring to think what it meant. Not yet.

The promise of the strip of green and blue was broken when two figures, a man and woman locked in a death struggle, catapulted across the lawn, then out of sight. Slow to begin with, my steps slowed even more; as I watched that slim postcard of world in front of me, I began to pick up sounds that seemed strange and unearthly to my underground-prisoner ears: the diminishing shouts and cries of open-air conflict, the unmistakable pop of gunfire. When I reached the end of the alley I jumped in surprise, seeing where we were: just beyond the strip of grass was the edge of the village square. None of us would have guessed that we were that close to the center of the Compound. I looked behind us to see that the old hospital we'd emerged from was barely visible from here, most of its bulk built against a hillside that sloped out of sight. This old, torturous world, this square with its scattering of gravel, the modest clapboard buildings that didn't do much to muffle the male screams from within—it was all different now, filled with shouts of war as small groups of men and women struggled hand-to-hand. In the middle distance I saw that several women had pinned down a man I had thought of simply as The Toucher—he was one of the most eager ticklers, pushing to the forefront wherever a victim was being tortured, making sure to get his licks in—and were tickling him to death. It was a gratifying sight, till I realized that the same fate awaited us if we got caught by any of his cronies.

"Which way?" Pollux yelled.

"What?" I turned and looked at B, Vega, and Pollux. It was the first time I saw Vega in the light of day—how small he was! And though I had seen B and Pollux in the light before, I was unprepared for how haggard they looked now, as haggard as I had looked that time when I caught my reflection in a glass door and couldn't tell myself apart from the Lost Ones. Then there was B's wound, a splash of crimson on his side now, the red undeniable even on that stiff gray cloth. Altogether this small group looked so vivid that it was as if I'd seen them before only in dreams, and couldn't find words for the astonishment I felt at seeing them in the flesh.

They just stared at me, open-mouthed, waiting for me to tell them which way to go.

"This way," I said, leading us, for want of a better idea, toward the front entrance of the Compound and the long dirt road that had brought us here. I had no eye for anything else, not even the conflict taking place all around us. We were meant to escape, and by God we were going to do it. I found myself walking, then jogging, then running, astonished again that I could find the energy to move so fast. Behind me, the other three were keeping up—even B, though he was limping on his wounded side.

The wide green lawn led to an open gate, then the dirt road.

And nothing else. No obstacles. No guards, no rednecks with machine guns. No Michael Loomis tearing up the road in his blue truck. *No danger.* I began to slow down, to give my aching ribs a break. "B?" I called behind me. "Do you feel free?"

I looked to see him grinning, despite his pain and the smear of blood on his face. That grin was the best thing I'd ever seen; I wanted to remember him that way, always. And when his eyes focused behind me and his grin faded, I wanted to deny what I had to take in then—the disappointment and fear twisting his mouth into a wreckage of hope.

I followed his line of vision, straight down the dirt road ahead of us. The one threat that I'd forgotten, the one I should have been fearing the most, was standing right there, not a hundred feet away.

A wiry little man naked from the waist down, his arms and torso wrapped in a straitjacket.

Dred Junior.

"He can't hurt us," I said. "He can't. There's just one of him and four of us."

B was right behind me, reaching for my arm. "Stop, man."

"There's no stopping now," I said, refusing to look at him.

"Stop, for Christ's sake."

I looked at him then. "There's four of us and one of him," I repeated.

B stared at me, wide-eyed, as if I was as frightening as that apparition ahead of us. He made several attempts to speak, his lips and tongue struggling to work together, to tell me, warn me.

I had no patience. "Come on!"

"W-wait."

"What for?"

"I remember." He stopped in his tracks. "Oh God, I remember!"

Pollux came up short right at B's shoulder. "What are you saying, man?"

B had tears in his eyes. "I remember what happened."

"It's all right," I said. "We'll get through this. We have to."

I had turned my attention from the road for just a few minutes, and now I was startled, looking back, to find that Junior had tired of waiting and had approached us instead. He spoke to me, chillingly, his voice seeming to originate in my own head.

You should listen to what your friend is saying.

"Go to hell," I said.

He laughed. *Now you're getting warm. Literally, if you'll take a moment to notice.*

Nothing about this man, this pathetic creature, could frighten or even concern me. I reached behind me for B's hand. "Come on. We'll just keep walking. We'll walk right over this piece of filth if we have to."

B didn't take my hand. I looked back and was astonished to see him falling, falling to his knees. Vega and Pollux were sinking also, all three of them on their knees now in the dirt, their clasped hands raised in supplication. Even the shadows they cast behind them seemed to be cringing.

"What are you doing?" I screamed at them. "*What are you doing?*"

Tears streamed down their faces—tears, or sweat, for it was warm, unaccountably so. Sweat ran into my eyes and I wiped it away with my dirty hand. All of my patience was gone.

You should listen to your friend, Junior said. *He knows. He remembers.*

I shook my fist. "I won't listen to another word you say, so help me God."

God's out of the picture, my friend. He has been for some time.

You see, the rest of your escape party knows what you're refusing to remember.

How absurd he looked, standing on skinny bare feet in the middle of the dirt road, his erection poking up between his thighs. "Out of my way," I told him.

All right then, here's a question for you: how do you suppose you ever escaped from me, down there in the cellar?

"I'll pound you into dust!"

Do you really not remember how you got out of my cell?

I wiped my forehead, this time on the sleeve of my coverall. Sweat ran down my back, soaking the coarse gray cloth. "I was taken away and put to work."

Yes you were. Because you made a deal, my friend.

I spat at the ground. The spittle vanished in a puff of smoke. The heat coming from behind me was so intense it was cooking the earth, baking the soles of my feet right through my boots. Of course, of course: the Compound was on fire.

Take a look behind you.

I didn't need to look: I could picture the rough clapboard buildings catching like tinder, flames curling above the flat tar paper roofs. And the old hospital, surely that was burning too.

Take my advice for once, and look behind you. My...rather famous friend doesn't like being ignored.

Yes, I was sure of it: the buildings were burning, fire crackling across the lawn. The children had escaped, had run to safety. The teenage boys, I hoped they'd gotten out too. And the women, and the other captives, if any were left. We would *all* get out. But right now I was so hot my skin couldn't breathe. I reached for the zipper-pull on my coverall and the molten bit of metal burned my fingers. I opened my mouth to tell Junior to fuck off, and my tongue seared, shrank to a cinder. Through no will of my own my head turned, finally, my eyes swinging round in nightmarish slow-motion to the real source of the heat, a ghastly red light.

EPILOGUE

Once you've misplaced the difference between sleeping and waking, it's hard to find it again. Consciousness is a blank screen at first, an awareness that my eyes are closed. And I'm not standing on baking ground but sitting at an angle, rather comfortably, my head supported. A bitter taste invades my mouth, irony curling along the edge of my tongue. I am not where I thought I was.

When I open my eyes I'm in my car, in the parking lot of the rest stop. Sweat has collected under my arms, in my crotch—the by-product of an overheated, unexpected sleep. I open my window and sit with the slightly cool air drifting over me. On the seat beside me is a tape recorder. Ahead, across an abbreviated lawn, sits the quaint little cottage where the rest rooms live. Is it true that I haven't been inside that building yet? I can picture it, though: the cold slate floor, the toilet stalls with their white louver doors. I take a deep breath, set it free, and for what may be only a moment I know everything.

My name is Rand. I went searching for the ultimate erotic experience and found more than I bargained for. I met the worst fate I could imagine, and sold my soul to the devil to escape.

My name is M-36, and I am a trusty at the Compound, a worker bee with a can-do attitude and my time in the Chamber at the beginning and end of each day to look forward to.

My name is Aldebaran, and I am hiding underground with other naked filthy men who have taken the names of stars.

Three states of being—none of them less unlikely than the others. I am all of these things, without knowing how or why. Drifting, perhaps liable to slip into any of these roles without notice. Trembling, I close my eyes again. When I open them I see, not Dred Junior or B or the angelic Crystal, but the little rest room cottage again swimming into view. I *am* here. There is no slippage in time, just a progression of events that runs its perfect circle again and again.

Any second now a blue panel truck will pull into the parking lot and pass slowly across my rearview mirror. It will be my first look at Michael Loomis, though I won't know his name yet. Then it will be time for me to leave the car, taking my tape recorder with me. As soon as I step outside, all of my foreknowledge will be lost. Locking the door, glancing around, I'll wonder if the man in the truck was looking at me.

I'll buy a bottle of iced tea from the vending machine and leave it sitting outside.

If it's true that I've slipped into a cycle that will run forever, always beginning now, then let it be a blessing that I have at least this moment of clarity. I know where I've been and where I'm going.

There's Michael, right on schedule—10:05 by my watch. Soon the watch will be taken from me, and my preoccupation with time will be useless.

I take the tape recorder in hand and crack open my car door.

I look across the roof of my car, farther down the parking lot, to try to see what's happened to the blue truck. It must have parked out of sight. Had the driver really looked at me, and if so, why?

Oh, my friend…

AUTHOR'S AFTERWORD TO THE 2024 EDITION

There are moments in any writing project that find me staring at the computer screen in a state of near hopelessness, trying to summon the words or an image that will inspire me to keep going. One of many such moments in the writing of *My Name Is Rand* can be traced to the first paragraph, where I struggled with the description of Granger's house. The breakthrough came with the image that the square white house, so bright in the afternoon sun, "seemed to hover a few feet off the ground." Somehow those words allowed me to keep going, searching for fresh observations, and feeling—regardless of what anyone else might think—that I was creating a work of literature.

More than twenty years later, when the book—published in 2004 and later discontinued, then published in 2010 and discontinued a second time—was to get a new life thanks to Tom Cardamone at The Library of Homosexual Congress (an imprint of Rebel Satori Press), it seemed like a simple task to dust the manuscript off and send it along. There were some edits to be made, though, in order to bring the text into compliance with current standards and practices. For example, when referring to race, "black" is now "Black." Also, there was some wording that I thought might be construed as insensitive to women, so I changed that. Considering the story contains kidnapping, murder, rape, and many more kinds of nonconsensual activity, you might wonder why I would worry about hurting some readers' feelings. It is a dichotomy: wanting to let *Rand* be as shocking and transgressive as it is, but also complying somewhat with the rules of a contemporary novel.

I was the luckiest writer in the world to have Ian Philips of Suspect Thoughts Press as copy editor on the first edition. The loving care he lavished on this most peculiar book was like a balm to my frazzled first-time-published novelist nerves. Meanwhile the publisher of Suspect Thoughts Press, Greg Wharton, spent time with me on brainstorming ideas for the cover and even the title of the book. (The working title was *You Know What to Do.* I had some brainy reasons for using that title, but Greg's suggestion of to just use *My Name Is Rand* was better. And the cover, designed by Shane Lukas, was a thing of beauty.)

Ian and I had some discussions about certain passages. One of these is the scene in which Rand meets Duke, in the strangely banal "break room" that looks like something from "some outpost of industry." The interaction between the two men stirs Rand's memories of his history with Black men, which is also a history of times and places:

As I watched him I saw all the other Black men I had known in my life. Lustrous dark skin in streetlight leaking through a pulled shade, or glistening in the dimness of a bathhouse room. Smooth curved dicks with heads brown, pink, or purple, swollen and ripe. Nipples clinging to a curve of muscle or hiding in coarse, tight curls. Navels like darker secrets within darkness.

In an earlier draft of this passage I had waxed even more poetic, taking the narrative on a quite a spin through Rand's memories. That instinct to *reach* for words and images had gotten the better of me. Ian helped me trim the passage so that in its final form it doesn't stray too far from the tone of the rest of the narrative.

The last example of heightened language I can think of comes from much later in the book, and again involves Duke, who is now known as Betelgeuse or (thankfully) B. After spending the night with B, Rand finds he is no longer "a lonely, disconnected consciousness but a force of creation, blazing through pitch darkness like a star." Whoa! What brought on this celestial magic carpet ride? This time the answer is obvious: Rand has just spent the night getting spiritedly fucked by a sex god, and vigorously tickled to orgasm as well. There are many scenes in the book in which we would not want to take Rand's place, but in this case I, at least, would be tempted to say, "I'm next."

Over the years, I've heard from readers (often through *Rand*'s Facebook group) from all over the world—England, Spain, France, Germany, Russia, Iraq, Iran, Brazil, Lebanon, Belgium, Brazil, Canada, China,Colombia, Indian, Iran, Israel, Italy, Mexico, and Russia. I thank everyone who is willing to climb aboard and take this strange, strange trip. All are welcome, and if they find more than they bargained for—well, that may be the most common experience for those who expose themselves to *My Name Is Rand*.

Wayne Courtois
November, 2023

The Library of Homosexual Congress, an imprint of Rebel Satori Press, preserves and promotes classic and provocative works of gay literature and nonfiction, with focuses on the AIDS crisis, the nascent gay rights movement as well as irreverent works of sexual culture and groundbreaking titles that deserve renewed attention.

Curated by Tom Cardamone and Sven Davisson